Spotswood, Virginia

by

Nancy Bourne

STEPHEN F. AUSTIN STATE UNIVERSITY PRESS

For more information:
Stephen F. Austin State University Press
P.O. Box 13007 SFA Station
Nacogdoches, Texas 75962
sfapress@sfasu.edu
www.sfasu.edu/sfapress

Managing Editor: Kimberly Verhines
Book design: Jerri Bourrous
Distributed by Texas A&M Consortium
www.tamupress.com

ISBN: 978-1-62288-408-7

TABLE OF CONTENTS

Memorial Mansion / 7

Dirty Dora / 16

Drawing Lily / 25

We Gather Together / 34

Sterling Silver / 46

The Columbia / 49

Green Spring Valley / 58

Going Under / 74

Faster Than A Roller Coaster / 84

Massive Resistance / 93

Acknowledgments / 137

for Henry

MEMORIAL MANSION

So there was my Jimmy sitting in the den, with his bare feet on the coffee table, watching the news on the TV. It made me happy just to see him, unexpected like that.

"You're home early," I said.

"You know what they're saying?" He jerked his head toward the TV. It was Governor Byrd talking.

I sat down beside him on the old blue linen sofa, which has gotten awful faded, and ran my fingers alongside his arm.

He pulled away. "All those integrationists up north? Governor says they'll be heading this way, making trouble down here."

"I don't think they'll come here."

His upper lip twitched.

"We got restaurants, don't we?"

That made me smile. "You calling that hamburger place out on River Road a restaurant?"

"Don't laugh. They mean to put their brown butts at restaurant counters."

"Don't tell Grandpa," I said.

He squinted at me. "Grandpa! What about you? They'll come to the library."

"I doubt it."

"Sure they will."

"They won't, honey. It's not a restaurant. Besides, they'll be marching in the cities, Atlanta, Birmingham, places like that."

"But if they come to the library, what will you do?"

I put my arm around my son's wide shoulders and stretched up to kiss his cheek. It's still soft, that cheek. "I'll cross that bridge when I come to it."

"I worry about you, Mama. I do. They're trouble makers, those outside agitators. You're so naïve."

"It's a library, honey, for children. At least my part is. They won't come."

"It's the Memorial Mansion, for God's sake."

"All the more reason," I said.

They called the public library the Memorial Mansion because of General

Lee. He was supposed to have spent a night upstairs in the blue room in a four poster bed when it really was a mansion, back during the War. The General had taken up old Harrison Langhorne's offer of a rare good night's sleep in that room when the Rebel troops were advancing or retreating, I can never remember which. When old Mr. Langhorne finally died at the age of 93, he left the place to Spotswood. The town fathers christened it the Memorial Mansion and turned it into a library. What else could you do with it?

"Shouldn't you be at work?" I asked.

He stood up abruptly and turned off the TV.

"Well?"

"I can't do it anymore, Mama. Crawling around on my hands and knees, shoving all those stinking feet into bargain basement shoes. I gotta find something more suitable."

I felt the old familiar tide of worry rising in my chest.

"Did you get fired, son?"

"They got this new girl, Liz something. Said they didn't need me. Anyway, I hated it."

I gave him a look.

"I'll get something better, something where you don't crawl around on your hands and knees."

I figured it would do no good to remind him how hard it was to find a proper job without a college education. No need to remind him of how many times his grandpa had pestered friends to take him on, to give him a chance. He knew all that. Nagging wouldn't change anything. He was twenty years old, and I loved him more than anybody in the world.

I work all over the library, but I prefer the children's section, maybe because I'm not much taller than the children. They put us in the basement, which would be gloomy except for the movie posters I've tacked all over the walls. *Treasure Island* and *The Secret Garden*. Makes things colorful. I love the smell of old paper and library paste, almost more than I love the books, and definitely more than I love the white marble statue of General Lee that lords it over the grounds out front of the Memorial Mansion. The mayor's nephew, who's an artist in New York City, got paid to create the statue, which is the General to the life, or so they say. For me, he looks pompous.

Now that Saturday morning, I was demonstrating the dinosaur exhibit I'd set up on the front table for several of the children, when something made me look up. A woman was just standing there, in the middle of the library, watching me. I was too shocked to speak. She looked to be about thirty, a clean-looking woman for all her dark skin, and she was wearing a blue-flowered cotton dress with large black buttons in the front. She didn't look like anybody's maid. None of those people are allowed in the library, except of course the cleaning lady and Harvey, the janitor. It's not that there's a "Whites Only" sign, like there is at the Spotswood swimming pool. Everybody just knows. And what I knew is I had to get this lady out of the library before somebody saw her.

"I'm sorry," I said when I finally found my voice. "But I'm afraid you can't use this library. There is a library over on Calhoun Street, and I'm sure it's open today." I spoke softly, hoping the children wouldn't hear me.

The woman didn't move. "I would like to use this one," she said. She spoke her words carefully, like an educated person.

"I'm afraid that's not possible." I walked to the door and held it open. Several of the children looked up, watching to see what she would do.

"Why?" The woman still didn't move.

"This is a whites only library," I said. I'd never had to say anything like that before. In Spotswood, those people know their place.

The woman looked at me out of scared, dark eyes. "I am a high school teacher," she said. "Here in Spotswood. And I need some books for my classes that are not in the Calhoun Street library. You have them here."

I could hear the children beginning to react. "Who's she?" "She don't belong here."

I had to act quick. "Look, Ma'am," I said. "Please leave. You're going to get into all kinds of trouble if you don't leave right now."

"I'll leave when I've checked out my books," the woman said. She was standing up real straight, like she belonged there, but her voice sounded squeaky.

"If you don't leave, I'll have to call the police," I said.

"Why don't you just give me the books? Then I'll leave."

I could see it was up to me. She wasn't going to budge. I knew I was much too small to force her out, and the adult part of the library wouldn't open for another hour. I considered phoning the cops, but I knew the local guy would call in all the squad cars and probably the fire department too, and there'd be no end of trouble.

"Look," she said, "all I want is *Great Expectations* and *Call of the Wild.*"

That made me stare. "Surely they've got those in the Calhoun library."

"Maybe they did at one time, but not now."

I knew right then it was the wrong thing to do, but I had to get her out of there, and nothing else came to mind.

"OK," I said. "But stand by the door while I get the books."

She smiled for the first time and I could see she was almost pretty in a sad sort of way. Her mouth was thinner than what I'm used to, and her hair had been straightened and was neat.

Meanwhile, I could hear the children talking among themselves, getting louder. The woman turned toward the children, and they broke off mid-sentence. I quickly grabbed the two books off the shelf, checked them out to myself and handed them over.

"Now, go. Please," I begged. "Leave the books in the return box outside, when you finish. Don't come back in here. Please."

The woman backed out the door, clutching the books. "Thank you," she whispered. "Hurry," I said. I don't know who was more scared, that teacher or me. I mean I would have lost my job if I was caught giving books to that woman, and we need the money. Not to mention I'd be bringing shame on my family.

"What's that woman doing in our library?" It was Dexter, of course. He's got no breeding, comes from the mill side of town. Some of the other children were staring at me, waiting for me to say something. "She was wrong to come," I said, as calmly as I could manage, because you can bet I wasn't calm. "But now she's gone. And don't you use that word, Dexter."

"What word?" He shouted that word again and again and again. I knew how to handle him. I took him by the arm and pushed him ahead of me out the door. "Come back when you've learned how to behave in a library," I said.

Daddy had barely seated himself at the head of the table that night when he shouted out, "Irma Mae, how come you let that bitch in the library?"

He gets more ornery by the day. My husband, James, looked up from serving the meatloaf and sighed. Jimmy stared down at his plate.

"How'd you hear about that, Daddy?" I asked, keeping my cool.

"Don't matter how I heard about it. Why'd you do it?"

"I didn't let her in. She walked in by herself. The door's not locked. I got her out."

"That's not what I hear."

"She's a teacher."

"I don't give a good goddamn what she is; she's got no right at all to set one toe in the Memorial Mansion." White flecks of spit clung to the corners of the old man's lips.

"Calm down, Daddy," I said. How many times in my life had I said that: *Calm down, Daddy.* I looked over at James, trying to signal him for some help. But he just smiled his tired old smile at me.

"Have some meatloaf?" he said.

"I told you it would happen," Jimmy said. "I warned you. You're in deep shit now."

"Watch your language, Jimmy," I said.

"You're acting like a goddamn fool, and you're telling your boy to watch his language?" Daddy stood up, knocking over his chair, and limped out of the room on his stiff knee.

We sat in silence, not looking at each other, taking small bites of meatloaf.

"He's right, Ma," Jimmy finally said.

"He's a bitter old man," I said.

"Everybody's talking about it. That kid from the mill is spreading it around town. I worry about you."

"Well, don't. I took care of it."

James reached across the table and patted my hand. "It'll be all right," he said.

Jimmy looked at his father with disgust. "It won't be all right," he said. "She'll be back, this schoolteacher lady, and Mama will let her in, and this town will go wild."

"Calm down, honey," I said. But I have to say, he made me nervous. It wasn't that I mind the folks who live in the Calhoun Street area using the library, especially the better class like that teacher. What's wrong with that? But it's against the law, and I'm not one to break the law.

A week passed. Mr. Talbot, the head librarian, demanded an explanation about what had transpired between me and the school teacher, and he warned me never to let her or anybody like her into the Mansion. I chose not to tell him I'd given the teacher books. I just prayed we'd get them back without anybody knowing who'd been reading them.

The following Saturday morning, I looked in the return box for the books, but no luck. That made me antsy, but I figured she'd bring them back sooner or later. I was re-shelving books, when I heard a commotion outside. Thinking the children were lining up, I unlocked the door and opened it.

There stood that school teacher, clutching the books tight to her chest, her dark eyes wide, begging. About twenty yards behind her, at least a dozen men were milling about on the grassy lawn. I figured Dexter's daddy had been watching for her. I tried to close the door, but she stuck her foot in and stopped me.

"Let me in, *please*," she whispered.

"I can't," I said. "I told you."

"Please," the woman begged.

The men moved closer. I knew some of them, Buck Poindexter who manages the Buick lot and Eddie Williams who pumps gas at the Esso station.

"Hey, Buck," I called out, "What's going on?"

"We're here to protect the Mansion from scum." But it wasn't Buck who answered. It was a man I didn't recognize.

I could see them moving slowly in my direction and some of them were yelling, "Keep the bitch out." "Whites only." It was a sorry sight. The teacher grabbed my arm with her free hand. Her eyes looked wild. "Let me in," she begged. "They gonna kill me."

I'd never been this close to a black person before. I could see the dark circles under her arms. I could smell the sweat on her. It was mixed with some gardenia kind of perfume. I felt like I was about to faint. Meanwhile, the men over on the lawn kept bellowing and coming closer. And I could see that a couple of them were carrying sticks.

I just couldn't leave her out there with all those riled up men. That's the truth. So I let her in and shut the door.

"Quick," I said, pointing to the stairs that led up to the main library. "You can get out that way."

But she just backed herself against the wall like a cornered animal and hissed at me. "Lock it. Quick. Lock the door." The words came in short, jerky breaths.

Now that I was inside the library, away from the crowd of men, I was appalled at what I had done.

"I can't," I said.

Then I heard the roar outside, getting louder. It scared me so bad I ran over and flipped the bolt. Immediately, the door began to shake; the knob rattled.

"Unlock that door," somebody shouted.

I looked over at the window. Someone was peering in. The teacher was cowering against the wall, still clutching her books with white knuckles. I didn't want to look at her.

I ran over to the desk and picked up the telephone.

"Who you calling?" the teacher whispered.

"The police."

"No. Don't. No. No." She was scared for sure.

But I had already stopped dialing and was staring at the window.

It was Jimmy's face, paler than usual, and he was frowning and motioning with his hand for me to come to the window. My first thought was, he's coming to help me. So I put down the phone and walked, in a daze, toward the window.

I raised the sill just high enough to hear Jimmy. His face was pressed close to the window pane. Behind him I could see the men standing out there on the green lawn, waiting. They were yelling something I couldn't make out.

"Unlock the door, Mama," Jimmy said. His voice was deep and calm. Like his dad.

"No," the teacher screamed. "Don't."

"I can't do it," I told Jimmy. "I'm scared of those men out there."

"I know, Mama," he said, "but I'm here. I'll protect you; you just gotta unlock that door."

I looked over at the teacher who was still clutching the books. "They'll kill me if you open that door," she said. "You know they will."

I looked back out the window. This time I saw Tony Watson from Jimmy's baseball team and Curtis Morris, the catcher. They were at church every Sunday. They weren't going to kill anybody.

Jimmy was pleading. "If you don't unlock that door, they'll break the window. I'm the only thing keeping 'em back."

"What's going to happen if I unlock it?" I asked.

"They won't hurt you."

I looked over at the teacher.

"What'll they do to her?" I asked.

"What do you care?"

She was standing up straight now, looking hard at me, like I was her only hope. "You got to believe me," she said. Her voice was squeaky, like it was when she had demanded the books and wouldn't leave. For just a moment, we stood there, that black woman and I, locked in that room together, both of us terrified of the yelling and banging outside.

Then she said, "They'll kill me," and looked right in my face.

And I said, "I know."

"I can't do it," I told Jimmy, turning back to the window. Over his head, I could see the men moving toward us. They were chanting something that sounded like "Whites only," and several of them were waving those sticks. Then somebody yelled, "Out of the way. Mama's boy."

Jimmy turned back toward the crowd. "Hell no," he yelled back. "I'm with *you*. I'm just trying to talk some sense into her."

Then they were grabbing Jimmy, pulling him away, knocking him down. Men I had never seen before. Big men. I started screaming. I don't remember unbolting the lock. I just remember the men, so many of them, streaming in the door, knocking down chairs, brushing books off the tables. All I could think about was Jimmy. I forced my way through those men, out the door, to my boy. I found him struggling to get off the ground, his face bleeding, his tee-shirt torn.

"You crazy Mama," he said. "You almost got me killed protecting that bitch."

"Hush," I said.

I put my arm around him and led him away from the crowd, back toward home. I could hear the whine of the police siren. Thank God, I thought. They can't hurt her now.

It wasn't until the next afternoon that I heard the teacher was in jail, charged with disturbing the peace and trespassing.

"What about those men?" I asked Jimmy. "What did they get charged with?"

"Why would they get charged?"

"Well, they beat you up." I looked him over. His face was scratched up, but otherwise he looked normal.

"I was in the way. Look, Mama, it's lucky they didn't charge *you* with anything."

"Me? Why?"

"You let that bitch into the Mansion. But, you're OK. I fixed it up," Jimmy said. "They won't touch you."

"How'd you do that?"

"I told the police she forced the door open and you couldn't stop her, then she bolted the lock."

"That's not what happened."

"That's what you'll say at the trial."

"I can't lie, Jimmy."

"Who says you got to lie? I was at the window, watching. I gave my statement. You're not gonna contradict me."

I didn't answer. But I felt sick all over.

The teacher's coming up for trial. They're expecting me to testify against her. Jimmy, the lawyers, the church, everybody. I keep seeing her, standing up so straight in the corner of the library in that blue flowered dress, looking hard at me with her dark eyes and hanging onto *Great Expectations* like her life depended on it. I can hear those men yelling outside and I feel the terror as that teacher and I stood locked together in that room.

I can't let her go to jail.

But then I think, she started it; she's the one that got me into this mess. And if I tell the truth about that awful day, that I opened the door to her and locked it, my boy will be in trouble. And all he did was tell a white fib to protect his mama. That's all he did.

But she's a teacher. All she wanted was books.

DIRTY DORA

I seen the papers. I know what they say about me, what they call me. Dirty Dora. Just because I danced one dance with one of them. Just one dance. This whole town's been in a tizzy ever since some fancy court said we got to go to school with them. So they make *me* out to be some kind of criminal and shut me up here in the courthouse. It ain't exactly a jail, at least there ain't no bars. But the door's locked, except when they bring me food or let my mama in to see me, which I wish they wouldn't, she's so shamed.

I been here a month, mostly in this room, sitting on this bed, looking out the window at the statue of Mayor Woods, white as chalk, up in front of the courthouse. Dead now. I ain't seen Trish or Faye since they picked us up, but I reckon they got them stashed away in rooms like this too. They supposed to get me a lawyer, but I ain't seen one yet.

Dirty Dora. It's not even my name, which is Doreen. But they don't care bout that. They just want to make a joke out of me, that's all. All those little pipsqueak boys in my class. The girls ain't a lot better. Much shorter than me with thin little arms and no chest at all. Some of them are nice though and ask me to draw things, horses mostly or girls all dressed up in pretty clothes.

One thing about being shut up in here, I don't have to go to school. I been going for eight years, seems like forever, and I never got no further than sixth grade. Had to repeat first. Then nasty old Miz Brown failed me in fourth. I'm fourteen now and stuck in sixth grade, second time around, and I can't read the science book or the history book or any of the books. I can do the arithmetic good as the boys, so long as they ain't written out problems. Numbers has always been easy for me. That's how I know I'm not dumb. But, since I'm no good at reading, they'll probably flunk me again. All I can say is, two more years I'm outa there. No more school.

Long about fifth grade I started changing. Got tall, got myself a bra. The other girls in my class stayed little, even the ones in sixth who had been in my class before Old Lady Brown flunked me. I could see them trying not to look when we changed clothes for gym. Funny thing was those same little girls were all friendly to me in gym class. We'd line up to choose sides for kickball, and whoever was captain would yell out, "I want Doreen."

"No fair. You had her last week," the other captain would say.

So they'd draw straws, and the long straw would get me. And good for them because we won every time. So I liked gym class. But I liked art best. You give me a subject and a pencil and some paper, and I can make it look so real. Dogs, cats, pretty girls with curved lips and long hair, like in the comics.

"Bet you can't draw a monster," Joey Kinser said just last month in that smart-alecky voice of his.

"What kind of monster you want?"

"I don't know. With fangs and stuff."

"Piece a cake," I said. Fact is, I could do it with my eyes shut. I'm that good. But I still hate that Spotswood Grammar School. Every time I had to read out loud, I'd say all the big words wrong and people laughed. I heard 'em call me Dumb Dora. Teachers too.

Back when I was in fourth my mama took off from her job at the Mill to see why I was doing so bad. She made me sit there while she asked Miz Brown straight out, "How come Doreen ain't moving up with her class?"

"I hate to tell you, Miz Harris," the old witch said, "but your daughter is behind in her reading."

"Well, whose fault is that?" my mama asked.

"I've done my best with her, but she just doesn't seem to progress."

"You think another year in fourth will help?"

"If she applies herself, I don't see why not."

But I been applying myself and it don't do no good.

"Why can't I quit Spotswood and go to beauty school?"

"Law says you gotta stay till you're sixteen," Mama says.

So I kept on going, kept on getting bigger. At recess when all the girls were playing hopscotch or jumping rope, I'd sit on the steps and draw pictures. That's how I met Trish.

She's this big red-headed girl who turned up one day during lunch period and sat down next to me on the stairs.

"You a good drawer," she told me after she been watching awhile.

"Thank you," I said. "You ain't in this school, are you?"

"Nope. I'm in seventh over there." She jerked her thumb toward the Junior High across the street.

"How come you over here?"

"I got permission to go home for lunch, but I usually mess around instead."

"Messing around at a grammar school don't sound like fun to me."

"Yeah. Well, I seen you over here all the time and couldn't figure out what somebody so grown up was doing at this baby school."

"I don't read so good," I said.

"Me neither," she said. "Draw me."

I looked sharp at her long carrot colored hair, her icy white skin, her purple dress bulging at the top with the biggest bosom you ever saw, and I said, "I need colored pencils for you."

Well, Trish rescued me. Mama says she ruined me, and I have to admit she got me into this mess. But I don't blame her. I didn't have no friends till she showed up. Early on, I'd had a couple of girlfriends at Spotswood Grammar, but they'd moved on to the junior high and didn't have nothing more to do with me. Anyway, Mama said they was trash, and maybe she was right. All I know is till Trish showed up, I was lonesome all the time. Mama was working the afternoon shift at the Mill and didn't get home till after I went to bed. I don't have no daddy; he joined the Army when I was a baby and never come back. There was another baby before I was born, but he died.

The drawing was what did it. Trish loved the picture I did of her with the colored pencils I borrowed from the art teacher. I say "borrowed" because I meant to give 'em back. Anyway, Trish had me draw a picture of her friend Faye in Green Street Park after school. Faye's a short little thing with a dirty blond pony-tail and skinny legs. So now I had two friends.

"You like dancing?" Trish asked me one day when we was smoking cigarettes in the park.

"Sure do," I said, although I had never danced a step in my life.

"You got a radio?"

"Yeah?"

"They play all kinda good music on WKRM. Elvis, Buddy Holly, Bill Haley."

"Sure do," I said, bluffing. What did I know? Mama told me she'd wear me out if she ever caught me listening to that dirty music.

"Let's go over to your house and do some dancing," Trish said.

"My mama wouldn't like that," I said.

"Is she home?"

"No."

"What she don't know won't hurt her."

"What bout your house?" I asked.

"My mama's home. You don't want to mess with her," Trish said. Faye nodded like she knew. "Come on, Doreen, let's go to your house."

I wanted to say no, but I didn't want to lose the only friends I had.

"Mama'll know if we leave a mess," I said.

"We won't leave no mess."

And we didn't. Most afternoons after school we'd have our smoke in the park. It was April and getting warm and it felt good to sit on the benches with my friends, like other people, and smoke our Camels. Sometimes the grown ups gave us dirty looks, but we just laughed. Then we'd walk over to my house, which is one of those houses the Mill rents out to its workers. They're all alike, wood frame, most of them needing a paint job, a little patch of grass out front. My bedroom is small, just enough room for a single bed and a chest of drawers. But the living room is big enough for dancing. We'd shove the sofa up against the wall and carry the two chairs and the rug into the kitchen. The rug was easy, just a small rag rug Mama made. Trish found the radio in the kitchen and turned on WKRM.

I'll never forget that first time. This voice was singing, "Get out from that kitchen and rattle those pots and pans," and Trish just started bouncing all over the room, waving her arms and singing. She grabbed Faye's hand and they bounced together, twisting and turning and laughing and singing. I hadn't heard that song before, which is hard to believe, but remember, I was in sixth grade with all those little kids.

"Come on, Doreen," Trish called out and grabbed my hand. I started hopping from foot to foot.

"Ain't you even been dancing?" she asked.

It was pretty obvious I hadn't.

"Come on, Faye," she said. "We gotta teach her."

They started me out just bouncing to the beat, not even moving my feet, just bending my knees up and down and waving my arms. Once I got the beat, they showed me how to move my feet. We practiced awhile, and pretty soon I got it. I got better and better at it. I didn't want to stop. Mama never guessed because we fixed up the living room good as new every time.

That summer Trish and Faye came over to my house every afternoon as soon as Mama left for work. We didn't always dance. Sometimes we played rummy or double sol. Sometimes we read love comics. One day Trish said, "I'm sick of dancing with girls. Let's find some boys to dance with."

"How do you mean?"

"I hear there's some dancing in the pavilion in Boyle Park," Faye said.

Trish perked up. "Yeah? When?"

"Friday nights."

"I can't," I said. "Mama won't let me." Truth is Mama played bingo at the church on Friday nights; she wouldn't know. But I was scared to be out in that park at night.

"Who's gon tell your mama?"

"Somebody might see me."

"Somebody's gon see you, alright, but they ain't the type to tell your mama."

I see now I was dumb to listen to her. But I loved that dancing. And, to tell the honest truth, I didn't know no boys and I was itching to dance with one. If I hadn't listened to her, I wouldn't have met Tommy.

It was August and steaming hot that first time, even at eight o'clock at night. Trish, Faye and I walked through the park to the Pavilion, talking and laughing real loud to cover up how nervous we were. I was wearing my white pedal pushers and those cheap ballet shoes that look like Capezios, and I was sweating under my arms. Once we got there, we hung around on the sidelines for a few minutes watching couples close dancing to *Love Me Tender*, which was playing on somebody's radio. I looked around to see if I knew anybody. I didn't and it made me feel easier.

Trish and Faye started dancing with each other, showing off, hoping to attract some boy's attention, which they did pretty fast. Then this soldier come up and asked me, real polite, "May I have this dance?" He was taller than me and had this blond curly hair and blue eyes. I mean I couldn't believe somebody so handsome was asking me to dance. *All Shook Up* was playing on the radio, and he took my hand and swung me out and pulled me back to him, his feet hopping to the beat and me right along with him.

"I haven't seen you here before, sugar," he said during the commercial break.

"This my first time."

"You in high school?"

I nodded. You couldn't tell a man old enough to be soldier that you're in sixth grade. "You in the Army?"

"Fort Dix."

"Where's that at?"

"North Carolina, about an hour from here. Name's Tommy," he said, "and if you have no objection, I'm gonna monopolize your company tonight."

I kept staring at him and breathing in a lemony smell like from shaving lotion and smiling like a big fool.

"Not much of a talker, are you, sugar?" he said.

"What do you want me to say?"

He laughed. "Anything you want to say."

"I can draw," I said.

He looked at me so solemnly. "Well, you have to draw me some time," he said.

I was having trouble breathing, he was so close. I wanted right then to draw him. I wanted to take my blue pencil and color in those deep violet eyes. I wanted to use the side of my pencil to shade in his cheekbones. I wanted to touch his ears that were so small and perfect. I wanted to feel the skin of his white neck against my mouth.

"I'm Doreen," I said.

I saw him every Friday night after that. We jitterbugged and slow danced. He would pull me right onto the front of his starched khaki uniform and rock me back and forth, whispering right in my ear, and every part of my body would be singing. We took breaks from the dancing, of course. Out in the dark where there were lots of trees. I let him do whatever he wanted, it felt so good. We didn't go all the way; I held him off there. But I wanted to. I still think about it. I loved that man.

Now here comes the bad part. School started and after a couple of weeks it got cold out there in the park. People stopped coming on Friday nights. But we wanted to keep dancing.

"How bout your house, Doreen?" Faye asked.

I thought about Tommy in my house, sneaking up to my bedroom, shutting the door. I almost said yes.

But then, "Too many people," I said. "Besides the neighbors would tell my mama."

"I know a place," this GI said. His name was Dwayne and I never seen him before.

"What place?" I could tell Trish was all for it.

"Called Dix Dance Club. Other side of town."

"What other side of town?"

He named a street I hadn't heard of. The cops don't believe me, but I had no idea.

"What's it like," I asked.

"It's a guy's living room. He got hundreds of records and he charges a dollar a person to let people dance there."

"How come I never heard of it?" I asked.

"Come on, sugar," Tommy said. "It'll be just fine. You know you want to."

He was right. I wanted to real bad.

So the last Friday night in September, Trish, Faye and I met Tommy and a bunch of soldiers in the park like always, only this time the soldier named Dwayne had a Ford car. We all squeezed in, the girls sitting on the boys' laps. We was so busy giggling and carrying on, I didn't pay no attention to where we was going.

"Here we are," Dwayne said as he slammed on the brakes.

There weren't no street lights, no lights in the houses, no car headlights even. It was dark.

"It's okay," Tommy whispered, kissing my ear. "You're with me." He pushed me off him and out the car.

Suddenly I heard *Peggy Sue* coming from somewhere and I seen Dwayne standing in the open door of one of the houses, motioning us to follow him. "Hurry up," he called out in a voice we could barely hear.

Now what choice did I have? We couldn't just stand out there in the dark.

Inside, the room was bare. No furniture. Shades over the windows. The floor was scuffed up and some of the boards was cracked. The only light come from a bulb hanging from the ceiling. And it smelled. Not real bad. Just like yesterday's dinner.

And then we saw them. Standing in a line against the wall, an old man, maybe fifty, two young ones about my age, and a small woman with a rag around her head.

They was dark as ink. All of them.

"We're leaving," Trish said.

We rushed back out the door, but Dwayne had gone off. Left us high and dry.

Tommy came outside. "Come on in, sugar. You can't stay out here. I promise we won't be here long."

"How we gon get home?" It was all I could think about.

"Dwayne'll be back. I promise."

I wanted to believe him.

What happened next I can't explain. One of thsoe boys put a record on the record player, which was in the kitchen, and the soldiers started dancing, first by themselves, turning and twisting and singing, then they was pulling Trish and Faye out into middle of the bare room. Tommy and I just watched. A few minutes later some more girls turned up, girls we'd seen dancing in the park. White girls. But they didn't act surprised like we was. It was like they'd been there before.

The old guy was handing out paper cups of lemonade, and we all started drinking it. We was thirsty. Now I know that it had something in it, but at the time I didn't even suspect. Tasted like lemonade. After a while, the beat of the music just got to me and I found myself hanging onto Tommy and swinging round the room.

Then I somehow lost hold of Tommy and he was dancing with Faye and it didn't even bother me. I just kept on dancing by myself. And then those dark skin boys was in the middle of us, shaking their shoulders and their hands in time with the music, moving their feet in a kind of shuffle. And the music wasn't Elvis or Buddy Holly anymore. It was this dirty song called *Work with me Annie* that WKRM wouldn't play on the air. But I'd heard about it. And I didn't know what to do with that dirty music and those boys shaking their hips and laughing. Then one of 'em grabbed my hand and swung me round so hard I got dizzy.

I was standing in the middle of the room, with that boy hanging onto me, crying out for Tommy, when the door burst open.

Mama says they gon send me away to reform school. Says they gon reform me so I never dance dirty again.

"What happened to that lawyer?" I say.

"He's the one got you reform school instead of jail," she says.

She keeps on crying every time she shows up.

"What'd I do wrong for you to turn out so delinquent?" she says. I reckon she got that big word from the newspaper.

"Weren't your fault," I tell her.

"It was them girls. They the ones made you so wicked. You stay away from them in that reform school. You hear me?"

"Yes m'am," I say, but I'm glad to hear Trish and Faye will be with me. Makes me less scared.

Mama says the cops only arrested the folks who were in the house that night, including all the girls. They didn't bother with the soldiers. I wrote to Tommy, but I didn't hear nothing from him. I figured the guards was throwing his letters in the trash. I missed him so much I started drawing him. They give me paper and a pencil and I drew him over and over. I said to those pictures, "Hurry up, Tommy. They gon send me away."

But he didn't come. Then I figured it out. Tommy's done with me; he don't really love me. He'd visit if he did. Or at least write. I try not to be mad at him, but he's the one put me in that man's house. If anybody's dirty, it's him.

I know I ain't. I may not be good at reading, but I ain't the Dirty Dora they talk about in the papers. And I can draw. Nobody can draw like me.

DRAWING LILY

They were out on the porch at the sun-bleached table, their heads close, almost brushing, the boy Julian chattering away, the grandfather Carl nodding, his narrow hazel eyes and full, chapped lips expressionless. Both had pencils and paper; both were drawing. Out of the corner of his eye, the old man saw his daughter, Ellen, pull a crumpled tissue from her pocket, then disappear into the dark pine-scented beach house.

Was she crying? He couldn't tell. And anyway, it made no sense. She'd known for months. Lou Gehrig's disease. There was a fancier name, but he could never remember it. And it somehow made him feel better that somebody famous, the baseball player, had died of it. Made the mumbling and the drooling he tried to conceal somehow less shameful.

He studied his grandson. Julian had his mother's high cheekbones and sharp chin. Her same colorless eyebrows and lashes; her lank blond hair. The boy was asking questions, staring at his grandpa's drawing, talking, talking as if his talking could fill the space left by the old man's silence.

"Is that Lily?" Julian asked, smiling at the cow his grandfather had drawn. A really good cow, not a milk-carton cartoon cow, but a lumbering field animal with lowered head and wet black nostrils and a bulging udder.

Carl's wiry, tapered fingers added the tail, filled in the black spots. He bit his lip and squinted at the paper. The lines in the translucent skin of his cheeks deepened as he concentrated.

"Tell me," Julian begged.

Carl shook his head and pointed at the boy's bare narrow chest.

"You want me to tell it?"

Carl nodded. He had told it so often, first to Ellen when she was Julian's age, over and over, and then to his grandson.

"She was a good milker, Lily," Julian said, imitating the slow, flat cadence of Carl's southern speech.

The old man smiled, revealing a dimple that quickly disappeared into the deep lines of his cheek. He pulled a handkerchief from his pocket and patted his mouth.

"Your papa got her at the county auction and he was right proud of her. You had to fetch her from the pasture every night before dinner." The boy paused. "How old were you?"

Carl pocketed the damp handkerchief and held up both hands, fingers extended.

"Ten? Like me." Julian paused for a minute as if to let that piece of information sink in. "You were worried you'd be late that night, weren't you? Your mama didn't like you to be late for dinner. You were standing up close to Lily about to take her lead rope when something spooked her. Something loud. And all of a sudden she just took off down the hill. You felt a powerful tug on your leg, then a stab of pain that knocked the breath out of you."

Carl smiled at the boy's recollection, not just of the story, but of the exact words Carl always used in telling it. Words like *fetch, spooked, powerful tug.* Words from the hill country near Spotswood, from the farm.

"Then you fell flat on your face with your left leg twisted under you." Julian stared down at his own skinny legs poking out of his bathing suit.

"You had managed to tangle your leg up in that lead rope without knowing it, and Lily had yanked you over when she charged down the hill."

He imagined he could still feel it. Luckily the rope had slipped off early on and he hadn't been dragged far. He had rolled over on his back, hollering out, trying to get up. But every time he tried to put weight on his left foot, the pain shot up his leg so bad he had to give it up. He lay there on that hill, pitying himself, for what seemed like hours, sure that Papa or Willard would come looking for him.

"You were all by yourself and nobody came." Carl felt the boy's hand, warm on his back, protective.

Nobody came. After a long time he got up on his hands and his good knee. He could still feel it, the sharp knife of pain as he dragged his hurt leg behind him up the hill toward the house. About halfway up he found a stick strong enough to bear his weight. He fell a time or two, calling for his mama. But finally he opened the kitchen door and crawled inside. She was washing dishes. She took one look at him and screamed. All the family ran in from somewhere and just stood there staring at him. Then Papa picked him up and carried him to the front room and laid him on the couch.

"Your mama was scared you had broke your leg," Julian continued. "But they didn't take you to the doctor, did they?"

Doctors cost money they didn't have, so they put it off. And next morning he was feeling better, except every time he tried to stand up the pain was so sharp he had to hold his breath to keep from crying out. So they let him stay on the couch for a week or so.

"But it didn't get better."

It felt a little better. Papa said it was a sprain and it would take time to mend. Told him to take it easy. But there was work to do. So when he could stand it, he got up and hobbled around as best he could. But it kept hurting and after another couple of weeks, he knew something was wrong. Not just a sprain. He'd had his share of sprained ankles. They hurt in a particular place when you moved a particular way. Papa would ask him where it hurt and he'd point to the place. This pain wasn't like that. It was all over his leg and it hurt all the time. There was no way he could move to get away from it. When it got that bad, he couldn't even get out of bed. Mama kept asking wasn't his leg getting better, but he told her it was about the same.

He couldn't remember much of what happened next, except that in the middle of the night his mama got out the truck and drove him to Spotswood, to the hospital.

"The doctor said you had a bad break. And he had to break your leg again before he could set it. He said the bones had started to knit back together crooked and you'd have been a cripple if they'd left it like that. How'd they do it? Break your leg?"

Carl walked across the porch and picked up a pine twig that had fallen into the sand. He snapped it into two pieces.

"Wow!" Julian breathed. "They knocked you out with ether, didn't they? Then they put you in a cast from your hip to your toes for six months. And you were on crutches for longer than that. After that you limped for years and years."

Carl was drawing again. This time a boy with his mouth turned down, walking on crutches.

"That's why you never played baseball." The boy thought for a moment. "Did Grandpa say he was sorry?"

The old man laughed and shook his head. Not a chance. His papa had said he was a damn fool to let that cow tangle his rope 'round his leg. They didn't have the money for doctors and the bad leg set them back considerably.

"But you got well, didn't you?" The boy was no longer imitating his grandpa's southern cadence. His voice was urgent now, insistent. "Your leg's perfect now, isn't it?"

Carl ran his hand through Julian's silky blond hair and kissed the top of his head, breathing in a mix of salt and sweat. He nodded.

"You got well," Julian repeated.

They picked up their pencils and began drawing again.

He could still draw anyway. Lou Gehrig hadn't robbed him of that. That's how he thought of his disease, as a personal tormentor.

He'd first noticed it a year ago, in the spring. That he was slurring his words. His daughter kept after him to speak more clearly, and he tried. But his tongue didn't work the way it always had and his throat felt tight. He tried to ignore it; he'd never been much of a talker anyway. But his daughter Ellen made him go to the University Hospital in Charlottesville for some tests. The doctors there told him.

So he was going to die. They didn't say that. They talked instead about medicines he could take to slow the process. They told him that the rest of his body, the parts that weren't his throat and tongue, were still sound, but he might need physical therapy. He could still draw pictures and write words even though his voice would soon be silenced. They didn't mention what he'd already figured out, that he would eventually lose the ability to swallow, that before it was over he wouldn't be able to breathe.

In some ways it was a relief not to talk. He didn't have to discuss his symptoms with Ellen, who watched him, birdlike, fear deepening the lines between her eyes. He could get on with the parts of his life he had always loved.

This summer, for instance, he had rented this cottage at the beach for a month, the way he had always done. Year after year when his wife Jane was still alive, and later with Ellen and her family. Only for the first time, Max wasn't here. The discarded son-in-law he continued to love even though Ellen no longer did, the missing father Julian telephoned every night but never talked about.

Carl could still take short walks on the silky white sand on legs that were functional, if not strong. He could roll up his pants legs and wade in the sunbaked ocean.

And he could draw, the way he always had, with confident strokes of the pen, with reckless joy. He was a draftsman by trade, had spent his years working in an architect's office. He sat now on the front porch of the cottage at the picnic table, with Julian, drawing. The noonday heat swirled off the sand in front of him, distorting the string of cottages that followed the curve of the beach.

Carl was absorbed in his drawing when Julian jumped down from the porch onto the hot sand and headed off in the direction of the surf. Every few minutes the old man shaded his eyes with his hand and looked out over the stretch of inert bodies clogging the shorefront. He could make out Julian standing about fifty yards away at the edge of the water, facing the panorama of surfboards, floats, girls in bikinis, splashing children. He knew Ellen didn't let Julian go it alone, but he trusted the boy to stay safely on the beach. At the same time he knew how much Julian loved the water, loved running into the crashing waves and being knocked under, loved feeling the heavy water rolling over him, the sand scraping his skin. Together they had been knocked over countless times, but they always bounced back to the surface, laughing, spitting out brine. Carl knew the ocean current was unpredictable. Knew that on rare occasions an undertow could carry you out without warning. But to him the ocean was familiar, warm, playful.

And then Julian was gone. Carl pulled himself to his feet and peered out into the shimmering sunlight, searching the spread of red and yellow beach towels where Julian had just been standing. He wasn't there.

Carl looked around for Ellen, but the cabin was empty. He thought he remembered something about her going shopping, but he wasn't sure. At any rate she wasn't here.

Panting heavily, he scrambled down the weathered porch steps onto the hot sand, weaving clumsily through the baked bodies strewn out on towels, through the children splashing water onto sand castles. At the water's edge, he peered out beyond the swimmers, scanning the waves for this most precious of boys. No Julian.

I won't panic, he told himself. He's somewhere on the beach.

A man, deeply tanned with wind-blown white hair, approached. "You OK?"

Carl mopped the saliva running down the ridges beside his lips with his crumpled handkerchief. "My boy," he mumbled.

The man peered at his face. "How old?" he asked.

Carl held up both hands, fingers extended.

"Ten?"

Carl nodded.

"Look, I'm sure he's okay. The current's been moving sideways up the beach. No undertow. Your boy's probably having too much fun to notice."

The man paused. "He's not alone, is he?"

Carl didn't answer but headed up the beach in the direction the man pointed, splashing the shallow water, pounding deep footsteps in the wet sand. His breath was ragged and his throat burned. Every minute or so he had to stop. He scanned the surf, his hand shading his eyes from the blinding sun. There were so many people out there in the waves. Too many. Had he missed him in all those bodies? Beyond the waves the water was black and vacant. Not a soul. He tried not to think about that.

He told himself that Julian was too sensible to swim by himself, too cautious. He tried to pick up his pace, glancing wildly around, but he stumbled and fell to his knees. A woman, too large for the bikini she was wearing, pulled him clumsily to his feet.

"Julian!" he tried to call out, but the word came out jumbled, broken.

"Are you alright?" she asked, her round face close to his, frowning.

He shook his head and tried to run, but he was unsure about the direction he should take, so he stood there in the hot sun, looking everywhere, seeing nothing. So that he almost missed him when Julian came wandering up the beach, his thin sunburned shoulders shaking from the cold water, strands of his wet hair streaking into his eyes.

"I'm okay, Grandpa. I'm okay." The boy grabbed him by the shirt and plunged his wet face into the old man's soft chest. Carl could feel his slight body trembling, could feel the tears.

"I know," he tried to say but couldn't. And so he wrapped his arms about the boy and held fast for a long time.

That night Carl sat with Ellen on the stiff mattress next to Julian who was absently picking up the colored pens and paper that floated over the surface of the lightweight summer blanket. The room was just large enough for the bunk bed and a small chest, and, like the rest of the cottage, smelled of pine.

"Why did you do it?" Ellen asked.

"What? Do what?"

"Go out there by yourself? You know better." Her voice carried an edge of anger.

"I know," he said.

"Then why?"

She took his face in both of her hands and looked him in the eye.

"I don't know. I meant to stay on the beach. But then I was in the water. And a big wave came and I couldn't touch bottom." He started to cry. "I'm sorry."

Ellen put her arms around him and held him against her. "What happened?"

"I was drowning," he said, his voice breaking.

"How did you get back?"

"I don't know. I was on the bottom. It was dark and the water was in my nose."

Ellen rocked him in her arms. The anger was gone. "You're safe now," she said.

Carl put his arms around his daughter and cradled both of them against him. His eyes stung from all the things he knew and couldn't say.

Julian pulled away from his mother. "This is going to sound weird," he said, "but I have an idea about heaven."

"Heaven?"

Carl was surprised. He couldn't remember the subject of heaven ever coming up before.

"I don't know. It's just an idea I got."

"Okay."

"Well, not exactly heaven. But a place you go, you know, after you die."

"Yeah?"

"Here's my idea. You go there sideways. Not up like heaven or down like hell. But somewhere different, and you go there sideways." He was fiddling with the colored pens, avoiding his mother's questioning gaze.

"Okay."

"Do you know what I mean?" He faced his grandpa.

Carl shook his head. He stroked Julian's cheek. It was so soft, so smooth. His beautiful Julio.

"It's a world like this one and you meet a lot of people in that place, your family and people you knew a long time ago."

His eyes were fixed on Carl's, silently pleading.

"It's a lovely idea," Ellen said.

"I don't want it to be lovely. I want it to be true. I want Daddy to be there all the time and you and Grandpa."

Carl pulled the boy to him, felt the soft flesh of his shoulder, felt his resistance.

"It's a lousy idea," Julian said, breaking away from his grandfather and sinking down into the covers.

Ellen bent down to kiss him. "No," she said, "It's a beautiful idea. I wish I could tell you it was true. I wish it were true. And maybe it is."

"Forget it," he said and turned away from her.

The next day they were back on the porch, each absorbed in his own drawing. And Carl had once again, without meaning to, drawn Lily. But drawing wasn't enough; he wanted his voice back. He had things to say. Things his grandson needed to hear. And sitting there, mute, impotent, he had drawn the cow. As if to remind himself, not of his broken leg and the months of wearing a cast, or the years of limping, or of sketching the baseball players he watched from the sidelines. But of something else, a memory he had pushed away, of lying in bed under a feather quilt in an empty house. Aching not just in his leg, but in his whole body. Shaking with cold in the warm spring afternoon. Calling out to his mother. But there was nothing, only silence, and he knew it was too late. They wouldn't get back in time.

He had no memory of their finding him, shivering, burning with fever, no memory of the ride to the hospital in the pickup. They had told him that part. What he remembered now, what his body remembered was the tightness in his throat, the sharp sting behind his eyes, the crush of darkness, the terror. No light anywhere, even from the window where the shades had been drawn. He called out, "Mama, Mama!" Silence. He held his breath, listening. Nothing. And he knew, right then he knew, he would die.

His hands were shaking and the space behind his eyes stung. To keep from crying, he looked over at Julian, absorbed in his drawing. This, he thought, this boy. He was what it was about, what he would miss. This very boy.

Carl ducked his head and reached for his handkerchief. Then he began to draw. A series of pictures, cartoon-like, of waves. Blue waves, black waves. They covered the entire page. Then there was a head, just a small head, barely visible above the breakers. He added a new frame to his cartoon. The head belonged to a boy. His arms were waving. Over his head was a moon, and a cow, just like Lily, was jumping over the moon.

Julian put down his own pencil and began to watch his grandpa. In the next frame, Lily jumped down to the ocean and started swimming toward the boy. A balloon came out of the boy's mouth, "Help, help, I'm drowning." The cow was getting closer.

"Grandpa," Julian laughed. "Cows can't swim."

The cow stopped swimming in front of the boy and wrapped the chain from her neck around the boy. She then began swimming back to shore towing the boy behind her. When he was safely on shore, the boy got up on Lily's back and rode off down the beach.

Julian laughed. "That's awesome, Grandpa. Do another one."

Carl placed a fresh piece of paper in front of Julian and pointed to him. And Julian began to draw.

WE GATHER TOGETHER

Last Thanksgiving my uncle Charlie shoved a newspaperman who was taking pictures in front of our church and knocked down his camera. His picture was on television, Uncle Charlie leaning over the man, his face just furious. At the edge of the picture you can see a policeman, all blurry, running up to stop the fight. What you don't see are all the people from Preacher Martin's church, dressed to the nines. They disappeared, just like that, before you could turn around. I know. I was there.

It's what comes of trying to integrate, my daddy said. He was dead set against it when the Reverend Coleman announced his plan a month or so before. He stood up in the pulpit and told us he had invited the Preacher Martin's Baptist church to worship with us on Thanksgiving Day.

"I got nothing against those people," Daddy said. "But they got their own church. It's a damn fool idea to try to mix them in with us."

And Uncle Charlie said, "I don't care what those Communists on the Supreme Court say, I don't integrate. I never will."

Some of the men decided to talk to the Reverend, bring him to his senses. I know because my daddy was one of them and told me all about it.

"The Court meant for schools to be integrated, not church," they told the Reverend. "Those folks will feel uncomfortable mixing with the professional people we got here at First Baptist."

But the Reverend just smiled. "Remember what you used to sing in Sunday School? Red and yellow, black and white, they are precious in His sight."

"Bible says nothing about mixing," the men said.

"We all worship the same God; we're all Baptists. It's time we came together in thanksgiving," the Reverend said.

I didn't know what to think. I was fourteen, and the only ones of them I'd ever known was Luther, the janitor at our church. They say Mr. Huntsman, the mayor's father, was his daddy, which is why his skin is so light. But of course that doesn't make Luther white. I've seen the maids on the back of the bus on the way to work, and the garbage men. But I don't *know* any of them. We don't have a maid; Mama and I clean.

When I first heard we had to go to school with the black kids, it scared me half to death. The white boys in my school are rough enough without having some boys from Calhoun Street fighting and talking dirty. And everybody says they're a lot dumber than we are. But it's been a couple of years since the Supreme Court said we had to integrate, and so far nothing's happened to change the schools. So I couldn't understand why the preacher wanted to make trouble at church.

On the other hand, I've always looked up to Reverend Coleman; everybody does. I consider him as good a Christian as a man could be. Maybe because he's always so nice to me, calls me by my name, Shirley, compliments me when I play the piano at Sunday School. He always stands real straight in the pulpit and opens up his arms like the painting of Jesus, telling us that God will forgive us no matter how nasty we behave. And when it's time for hymns, he throws back his head and sings louder than anybody. So when he asked why God would want us to turn a family away from our church just because I didn't know what to think.

Every Sunday until the big day, Reverend Coleman read the parable of the Good Samaritan to make his point. And he wore down most of the deacons and some of the women with his arguments. Not my mama, of course; she always sided with my daddy and Uncle Charlie. And they were against it. But they got outvoted.

Uncle Charlie is the President of the Spotswood Bank and the Chairman of the School Board. He's always been my favorite uncle. He doesn't have any children himself, so he's made my brother Sonny and me his substitute children. Uncle Charlie laughs a lot, and he brings me Hershey bars, and he once gave me a little bronze statue of the Empire State Building, which he had bought in New York City. He's very handsome with lots of wavy red hair, not like my daddy who's almost bald.

But mostly he's my hero. Like the time we were at a Lion's Club picnic on Luna Lake, and Daddy and Uncle Charlie took us out in a rowboat. Sonny was only two and of course he couldn't swim, so Mama said he couldn't go. But Sonny kept climbing into the boat and smiling at Daddy. So when Mama wasn't looking, Daddy pushed off.

I put my hand in the water to feel the cool on such a hot day and watched the ripples coming out from my fingers. I liked looking at Uncle Charlie's shoulders while he did the rowing. They were full of muscles and getting red from the sun. He's much stronger than my daddy whose shoulders are thin and bent forward. Maybe from bending over the cash register at the store all day.

All of a sudden I heard a splash. I looked around, but Sonny wasn't in the boat. And he wasn't in the water. I started screaming.

Then another splash and the boat started rocking so bad I had to hold on with both hands. It was Uncle Charlie. He'd jumped in. Daddy was yelling and I could hear Mama calling us from the shore. It seemed to go on forever. Once in a while my uncle's head would burst out of the water, his red hair plastered to his forehead, and then back down he'd go. Finally, he pulled himself into the boat, which was rocking so bad I was afraid it would go under. He flopped down on his back, soaking wet. Sonny was spread out on top of him like a rag doll. They lay there without moving while Daddy was pulling at them and I was screaming and screaming. Finally Sonny opened his eyes, slowly, like in a dream, but he wasn't looking at anything.

"Row!" Uncle Charlie yelled, "Row!" He picked Sonny up and hit him hard on the back. Nothing happened. Then he laid him down on the seat and put his mouth on Sonny's face. I watched him breathe into my brother's mouth, then suck the breath back in. We were all quiet now, waiting, and Daddy was rowing hard. When we hit shore, Mama jumped into the water, sun dress, sandals and all, crying, "Where's my baby?"

Uncle Charlie didn't look up; he just kept breathing for Sonny, hunched over him, wet and white and serious. All of a sudden, Sonny wiggled. Then he started choking and crying and spitting up water, but he was breathing for himself.

Daddy grabbed him and wrapped him in a beach towel. Mama was crying and hanging on to Daddy. I hugged Uncle Charlie, and he put his arms around me.

Daddy insisted that we leave for church right after breakfast that Thanksgiving morning to make sure we'd be seated down front.

"Don't want to sit behind the them," he said.

I didn't want to go. But Daddy made me. He said, we'd always gone to church on Thanksgiving and nobody was going to keep us away. You know what I mean? So I put on my brown felt hat with the veil, which Mama always made me wear to church, and my white gloves.

The church slowly filled up with folks we knew until it was about five minutes before the ten o'clock service was to start. The organ was going full tilt with *Onward Christian Soldiers.*

"Looks like we're safe," Mama whispered.

"Not a chance," Daddy whispered back.

They were walking in a bunch down the side aisles, the men in dark suits, the women all dressed up in bright colored dresses, red and blue with big flowers, and feathers waving off their hats. They didn't look like maids or janitors or garbage men. The girls in pigtails and stiff little skirts faced straight ahead as they followed their mamas down the aisles, hanging onto their hands. The boys were all in suits. I didn't see Luther anywhere.

"All rise."

It was Reverend Coleman. He had slipped in when I wasn't looking and was standing in the pulpit, his arms spread out, that big smile on his face. Next to him stood a tall, fat man, with rough skin the color of dark chocolate, Preacher Martin, I figured. He had on this light blue suit and a red tie, but he wasn't smiling. He didn't even look at us; he kept his eyes on his hymn book, which was open in his hands. I figured he wanted to be there about as much as I did.

Reverend Coleman spent a long time welcoming everybody to our church and saying what a glorious Thanksgiving Day God had provided. He said a prayer and then the organist belted out *We Gather Together To Ask the Lord's Blessing,* and the choir joined in. The church was full of people by this time, all the white people in the middle, Preacher Martin's people on the sides, so you would think we'd fill up that place with singing. But the sound was pretty pitiful. I didn't feel like singing, and I guess the other people felt the same. But I could hear Reverend Coleman's voice, deep and steady, way out in front of everybody, *"He chastens and hastens His will to make known."* I couldn't hear Preacher Martin, but his lips were moving.

After the hymn, the service proceeded as usual. The choir sang, the deacons from both churches passed collection plates, Preacher Martin read the Beatitudes from the Bible, and Reverend Coleman preached about "Blessed are the peacemakers." Except that were were what you might call integrated, it didn't seem much different from other Thanksgiving services.

Every once in a while, I'd look over at Uncle Charlie. He was sitting on the front row with the other deacons, but kind of to the side, so I had a good view of him. I noticed he wasn't singing during the hymns, which was unusual for him; he loves to sing. And whenever either Reverend Coleman or Preacher Martin started talking, he looked down at his lap.

During the last hymn, Reverend Coleman walked up the aisle through the congregation and waited at the door to greet people as they filed out. I started to join the line.

But Daddy said, "Hold on there, Shirley. Let *them* get out first."

By the time we got to the preacher, the church was nearly empty. I shook Reverend Coleman's hand and started down the stairs in front of the church. Then I stopped. The yard below was packed with people. Some I'd never seen before. And there were cameras everywhere. Big boxy cameras on stands with men crouching behind them. It was a mess. People were running away from the cameras, down Main Street, and men holding pencils and notebooks were running after them, shouting questions. I could hear them.

"How many black people were in that church today?"

"Who gave the sermon?"

"What was it like to sit next to them?"

Main Street was full of cars but they weren't moving, and all around and between the cars, all kinds of people were yelling that bad word."

Reverend Coleman rushed past me down the stairs into the crowd.

"These are religious people," he kept saying. "Let them pass."

But the newspapermen ran past him, bumping into him, paying him no mind.

"Back into the church," Daddy ordered. "We'll go out the back way."

I stood there.

"Shirley!" his voice was harsh.

"Uncle Charlie!" I cried. Because I had just seen him, in the middle of all those people.

"You got no right to take pictures of my church," he shouted and pointed at a cameraman who was focusing on a woman in a big red hat. She was looking all around like she'd lost somebody.

The man motioned for Uncle Charlie to get out of the way. But he didn't.

He walked over to the camera and with a loud crash knocked it onto the sidewalk. The cameraman started after Uncle Charlie. That's when my uncle shoved him and he fell.

"Shirley!"

As I turned back into the church, I heard the sirens screaming.

On the news that night they kept showing the picture of Uncle Charlie, leaning over a man, looking fierce, and the broken camera smashed beside them.

The TV announcer said, "Today, in Spotswood, Virginia, Charles Sherwood, President of the local Spotswood Bank, assaulted a *New York Times* photographer to prevent his taking pictures of the first integrated church service in the state of Virginia."

"Turn that thing off," Daddy yelled. But I kept watching. The man on TV was talking at the top of his voice, "Mr. Sherwood was arrested at the scene but was shortly released and is free on bail."

"Goddammit, I said turn it off."

Mama was sitting crouched over the kitchen table, her nose red and swollen. She still had on the hat she'd worn to church, the one with the black feathers. Daddy sat down beside her and put his arms around her.

"Don't you worry, sweetheart. Charlie will get off. He was just protecting our church. The judge knows him. He'll see it was self-defense."

"Why did he break the camera?" I asked.

"He didn't break the camera. The camera fell down while he was trying to keep those New York people from stirring up the crowd."

"But he knocked that man down," I said.

"Go to bed," Daddy said. "We'll talk about it in the morning."

For the rest of the Thanksgiving holiday, Daddy refused to talk about it. On Sunday, Reverend Coleman asked God to help us forgive those who revile and persecute us. I wasn't sure whether he meant the *New York Times* or all those people in the street, calling us names.

I didn't want to go to school the next Monday; I figured the kids would be asking me a lot of questions. But it turned out they were too busy arguing about whether or not Elvis's voice sounded dirty when he sang *Blue Suede Shoes*.

So when Mr. Jefferson, out of the blue, asked our Social Studies class whether we thought knocking over a newspaper camera was a violation of Freedom of the Press, I was stunned.

Henry Matthews waved his skinny arm in the air. "He shouldn't have done it. The newspapers have the right to record the news."

That got Barry Arnold going. "They shouldn't have let those freaks in that church in the first place."

Everybody had an opinion.

Mr. Jefferson started walking up and down the rows of desks, his head bent forward like he was listening, his hair hanging in his face, his pants dusty from chalk. Then he stopped at my desk. I sat very still.

"What do you think, Shirley?"

I looked up, scared. Did he know it was my Uncle Charlie who had knocked over the camera? I couldn't tell. But I had to defend him. So I said the first thing that popped into my head: "He had to do it."

"What do you mean?" He walked back to the front of the class.

"He was protecting the people at the church."

"Protecting them from what?"

"Those newspapermen were chasing the church people."

"Were you there?" Mr. Jefferson asked. He was looking at me like he was really interested.

I nodded.

"Would you tell us what you saw?"

Everybody turned to look at me.

"It was my Uncle Charlie," I said, "and he was protecting those people when they were coming out of church."

"Do you think that gave your uncle the right to knock down a news camera?"

I felt my face get really hot.

"You don't know what you're talking about," I said. "You weren't there." I was trying not to cry.

Well that started it. Everybody was yelling, blaming Uncle Charlie, blaming the church.

"Shirley, would you see me after school?" Mr. Jefferson said. Then he clapped his hands. "That's enough of Current Events. Open your books to page 45."

I ran out of the room before the tears came. I hid in a stall in the girls' bathroom until I heard the bell ring for the end of the period. Then I ran home.

Mama could tell something was wrong the minute I got home.

"It was Mr. Jefferson," I said.

"What about him?"

"He said some mean things about Uncle Charlie."

"What things?"

"I don't want to talk about it." I felt I was somehow to blame. I had talked back to Mr. Jefferson, which was a first for me, and I hadn't gone to see him after class. Plus I'd cut school. I was scared of what Daddy would say, but at the same time I was really mad at Mr. Jefferson.

So Mama let me be, but when Daddy got home from the store, he went after me until I told the whole story.

"The son of a bitch," he said under his breath. "He'll hear about this."

And then, to my surprise, he hugged me really tight and told me I had done the right thing. And Mama hugged me. And later Uncle Charlie came over and teased me about being his lawyer. I went to bed almost happy.

The next morning when we arrived at school, Daddy surprised me by parking and jumping out of the car.

"Come on," he said. "We're going to get to the bottom of this."

I didn't like the sound of that and made a beeline for my locker.

But he reached out and grabbed me by the elbow. "You're coming with me, honey," he said.

"I don't want to."

But it was too late.

Mr. Harrison, the principal, smiled at Daddy and shook his hand.

"Come on in, Earl," he said. "What's on your mind?"

I'd never been in the principal's office before, and I was surprised how messy it was. Textbooks were stacked on the desk, on the table, some even on the floor, and there were papers everywhere. We sat at the table on wooden chairs, Daddy and me on one side, Mr. Harrison on the other. I looked out the window.

Daddy started right in. "Rick, you've got a teacher here who's preaching integration politics in the classroom."

"Yeah?"

He turned to me. "You tell him what happened, Shirley."

Mr. Harrison is a short man, not much taller than the students, but he has these beady eyes that make you feel guilty, no matter what you've done, and he fixed those beady eyes on me.

"I don't want to get anybody in trouble," I said.

"You won't if you tell the truth, young lady."

So I did. I told him what Mr. Jefferson said about Freedom of the Press and Uncle Charlie. I didn't want to, but I did.

"You see?" Daddy said. "See what I'm talking about? Harassing my girl like that. You have to do something, Rick. That man has no place in the classroom."

"Thank you," Mr. Harrison said. "Why don't you go to class, Shirley?"

I was only too happy to do that. As I left the room, I heard Daddy say Uncle Charlie's name and something about the School Board.

There was a substitute in Social Studies that day. And Mr. Jefferson didn't turn up the rest of the week, which was a big relief.

At lunch period on Friday, Henry Matthews came over to where I was eating with my friend Sarah. His slide rule banged against the table as he leaned over me. "I hope you're satisfied, now that you got Mr. Jefferson fired."

"I did not."

"Well, your daddy did. He bullied Mr. Harrison into firing the best teacher we ever had in this dump of a school."

"You're lying," I said.

After Henry left, I asked Sarah, "What's he talking about?" But I knew and I felt sick to my stomach.

"I heard a rumor," she said, "that Mr. Jefferson was leaving, but it can't be your fault." She hugged me.

I could have told her the truth. About my talking to Mr. Harrison. But suppose it got out. Sarah's my best friend, but still, she might let it slip. And I didn't want anybody to know about it.

So I said, "I hate Henry Matthews."

It's January. Mr. Jefferson never came back. We've been having one substitute after another in Social Studies, and we haven't learned a thing. Even though I still blame Mr. Jefferson for what he did to me, I have to admit he made Social Studies interesting. Henry Matthews and his friends are still mad at me.

Mr. Jefferson isn't the only one leaving town. Reverend Coleman announced at the Christmas Eve service that he'd got the call to a church in Washington D.C.

"How come you're leaving?" I asked him last week. It was after choir practice and I noticed the light was on in his study.

"Hi Shirley," he said. "Come on in." He has a wonderful smile.

"Don't leave," I blurted out.

"I don't like leaving," he said, "but it's the right time. Besides, have you ever been to Washington?"

"No Sir."

"Well, you have a treat in store when you and your mama and daddy come to visit me."

"Is it because of Thanksgiving?" I asked.

He smiled again. "Is that what you think?"

"I guess so."

He was quiet for what seemed like forever. Then he said, "It's not your Uncle Charlie's fault. Don't think that for a minute. It's just time for me to go."

"I wish you wouldn't." I started to leave, but I needed to talk to somebody about Mr. Jefferson. Maybe that's why I went to Reverend Coleman's office in the first place.

"Mr. Jefferson is leaving too," I said.

He looked up, like he was surprised I was still there. "Mr. Jefferson, the teacher?"

"Yes Sir."

"Why is that do you suppose?"

"They say he got fired."

"That's pretty serious."

"He shouldn't have been talking about Uncle Charlie in class." It still made angry, just thinking about it.

The Reverend got up from his desk and put his arm around me. "Come over here, Shirley," he said, and sat me down beside him on this brown sofa he's got in his office.

"They say I'm to blame. That I got him fired." I could feel tears coming, but I held them in.

"How can they say that?"

I told him about Mr. Jefferson talking about Freedom of the Press. About how I had defended Uncle Charlie. About how Mr. Jefferson had treated me.

Reverend Coleman was watching me in such a serious way. "No wonder you're upset," he said.

I looked up into his face. "It's because of me he got fired," I said. My voice sounded squeaky. "Daddy made me tell Mr. Harrison what happened. And he got fired."

Reverend Coleman sat close, with his arm around me.

Finally he said, "You didn't do anything wrong, Shirley. One of these days you'll have to decide what you think about breaking cameras and Freedom of the Press, but whatever you decide, this wasn't your fault."

He gave me a hug.

"Do you understand?"

I nodded and stood up. I wanted to believe him.

Uncle Charlie came over last night to celebrate what he called his David and Goliath victory.

"How bout that, kid?" he said. "Your uncle whipped the mighty *New York Times*."

"You did?"

"You bet. They agreed not to press charges."

"Were they going to send you to jail?"

"I was never going to jail, sweetheart. Not a chance."

"Your uncle was a perfect gentleman," Mama said. "He offered to pay for the camera."

Uncle Charlie popped the cork off a bottle of champagne and poured glasses for him and Daddy. Mama, Sonny and I had orange juice.

"Let's drink a toast to Shirley." He winked at me. "She's rid this town of two trouble-makers."

I put my glass down. "Huh?"

"Your Mr. Jefferson's out on his ear. I made sure of that. And good riddance to Preacher Coleman."

"That wasn't me!" I cried out.

He picked me up and twirled me around. Laughing and laughing. I've always loved it when Uncle Charlie holds me up like that. But this time felt different.

"Put me down!" I shouted.

I struggled out of his arms and looked right at him.

"It wasn't me, it was you," I said. This time I didn't hold it in. I was sobbing. "You started it. And look what's happened. It's all a mess."

They were staring at me. Nobody was laughing.

STERLING SILVER

Even after all these years, Rosemary could still picture her cousin Beth, standing on the church steps, her veil swirling around her, her chin high, laughing. And Fred in white dinner jacket and tuxedo pants, clutching Beth's arm like he'd never let it go.

She'd been there. Fifty years ago. A member of the wedding. And she would go this time. All the way cross country to California. Because of the note tucked inside the invitation. *Rosie, dear, you really have to come. You're the only person besides Fred and me who was there. Beth.*

She'd been in high school. A clumsy bridesmaid, with unruly red hair, wearing light green taffeta, the bouffant skirt hitting her mid-calf, the shoulders tight on her bulky teenage frame. The dress, which she'd worn at her own courthouse wedding six years later, was now boxed up in the attic. Fading away, like her failed marriage.

But she'd been part of all that glamour. Wedding presents spread out on white linen for family and friends to admire and envy: sterling silver knives and forks, trays and pitchers, two complete sets of fine china, brocade table cloths, toasters and Mix-Masters. Luncheons and afternoon tea parties. Cheese straws and pink icing on the cupcakes. Rosemary had been there.

Five other bridesmaids, glossy and beautiful. Four hundred guests crowded into the Spotswood Golf Club. Nibbling shrimp and sipping punch. And she'd caught Beth's bouquet. A lone magnolia flower, pristine white petals, large shiny leaves.

Rosemary loved California, the flaxen hills, the windswept cypresses, the thundering Pacific. She loved the ruby red rhododendrons in Beth's garden, the purple salvia, blue hydrangeas, iridescent hummingbirds. And it all smelled so fresh. But best of all was Beth and Fred. They hugged her, flattered her, called her star of the show.

On the day of the party, Beth wore a long-sleeved blue silk dress, embroidered with seed pearls and topped by a matching cashmere sweater, her silvery hair shining. Rosemary shivered in her sleeveless, white lace, as the thick fog rolled in.

The country club ballroom was a confusion of noise and color: Orange Tiger Lilies in silver buckets on the buffet, vases of red and yellow roses on the smaller tables, bevies of coiffed blond ladies shouting over each other, children racing around, bumping into knees. On one wall, wedding photos flickered, interspersed with baby pictures and photos of beach and backpacking adventures. Fifty years of a marriage.

In Beth's welcoming speech, she introduced her cousin Rosie, the guest of honor, her bridesmaid. Everyone smiled and clapped. In that moment Rosemary no longer cared that her dress was all wrong and the hair shoved behind her ears was lank and gray.

"When I got married back there in the south," Beth continued, "lots of folks gave silver to the bride. And I collected my share." Her laugh was silvery. "But here in California, with a bunch of babies, I didn't have the time or inclination to polish the stuff. So . . ." She paused for effect. "I never used it. In fact, it's been packed away in the original boxes ever since. Now, fifty years later, I'm giving it away. As favors. So please help yourselves." She pointed to a table at the back of the room. And she laughed. And everyone laughed with her.

Rosemary joined the guests as they crowded around the table covered with shiny mint julep cups and pitchers, casserole dishes and ashtrays, little bells and serving bowls. The guests studied them, held them up to the light, giggled, compared and debated, then carried them off, remarking to each other that Beth was such an original.

"Look at this!" a woman in purple velvet exclaimed, picking up a wine goblet, its foot encrusted with elaborate silver roses, its stem entwined with sharp-edged vines. "Who could drink out of such a thing? It's so Victorian. It hurts my hand just to hold it."

"I know," Beth laughed. "God knows where it came from."

"Could I have it?" Rosemary asked.

"Oh, but I got here first," the woman said. She held her treasure up, turning it round and round. "I have to have it. It's so ugly, it's beautiful."

Still laughing, Beth stooped to pick up a folded piece of paper that had fallen out of the cup.

"Please give that to me," Rosemary pleaded, reaching for the paper.

But Beth had opened it and started reading. "Our great-grandmother . . ." She stopped.

"Go on," the woman in purple velvet said.

"Our great-grandmother Elizabeth Wilson sipped sherry from the cool thin lip of this silver goblet. I want you to have it."

Beth looked at Rosemary, her cheeks flushed.

The woman in purple velvet quickly set the goblet back on the table.

"Oh my God," Beth said. "I'm so sorry. I never saw this."

Rosemary stared at the ceiling, willing herself not to cry. "Mother and I found it in the attic," she said, speaking in a rush, "in a hatbox, wrapped in newspaper. I thought . . ." She reached for the goblet. "Look," she held it up and ran her finger along the side of the cup, her voice shaking. "It's engraved. See? It says *Elizabeth*."

And then Fred was beside her, wrapping his arm around her shoulders, folding a handkerchief into her hand.

"I want our friends to meet you," he said and, giving her time to wipe her eyes, he led her into the crowd.

She shook hands with the guests, one at time, while Fred told stories of the wedding and how Rosemary was such a big part of it. And Rosemary smiled and smiled and clutched her great-grandmother's silver goblet until her fingers ached.

THE COLUMBIA

Reva Hamm's big toe stuck straight up. No one in Spotswood suspected. They just thought that the bulky brown shoes she always wore were the style up north, where she'd gone after high school on a piano scholarship. Reva played like an angel, all the classical pieces and hymns. No show tunes though. But she didn't stay in New York after she graduated from Julliard. She just turned up back in Spotswood and practiced her piano pretty much all day. You could hear her out on the street. The hymns mostly. Sounded like she went through the whole Broadman Hymnal, end to end, at least once a week. People who saw her in town, carrying groceries in a faded cloth bag, picking up her father's starched white shirts at the cleaners, waiting for prescriptions at Johnson's Drug Store, said she was surely a treasure to her mother, who rarely left her bed.

But Birdi knew about the toe because she'd seen it. She was visiting her friend Mrs. Hamm in that second floor bedroom with all the windows shut and the blinds drawn. It was hot enough to melt, but the old lady had pulled the cotton blanket with the cornflower pattern up to her waist, and was propped up, as always, against three or four pillows in the four poster mahogany bed. Her gray hair was pinned into a knot on the top of her head and her face was white as flour and quilted-looking. Birdi sat on the stool close to the bed, her eyes fixed on the old lady. And they were both laughing out loud at the antics of the Banks family as Mrs. Hamm read from *Mary Poppins*.

"Time for your medicine, Mama." It was Reva, standing at the bedroom door, clutching a pill bottle in her hand, her voice shrill. She was wearing lime green shorts and a white pique halter; her limp brown hair was pulled back in a ponytail. And she was barefoot. Which is why Birdi stared. She'd only seen Reva in the brown shoes. The big toe on her right foot was stuck up straight as a ruler. The other toes were ordinary, just lying there on the hardwood floor flat as you please.

"Just put it here." Mrs. Hamm pointed to a small table beside her bed cluttered with crumpled up tissues and a couple of empty drinking glasses.

But Reva was giving Birdi a hard look. "Mama, you know you're not feeling well enough for visitors," she said.

"I said to put the bottle here." Mrs. Hamm's sharp tone startled Birdi.

"Now, Mama, the doctor said for me to administer your medicine." Reva shook out two small white pills from the bottle and handed them to her mother.

"What does he know? Put the bottle over here; I can count out pills myself."

Reva frowned, then placed the bottle on the table. She turned to Birdi. "Now don't stay long," she warned. "Mama needs her rest."

"Oh, I'm never too tired for my Birdi," the old lady said.

Reva stood beside the bed for a minute, her fingers twitching at her sides like she was playing the piano. Then, "Do you need anything else, Mama?"

But there was no answer.

After Reva left the room, Birdi interrupted *Mary Poppins* to ask, "What's the matter with her toe?"

"She's a musician, dear."

Birdi gave that some thought. Had she injured it on the piano pedals? But she didn't have time to pursue the subject, because Mrs. Hamm downed several pills with a glass of water and said, "Birdi, dear, I bet you'd like a bicycle."

And that's what Birdi wanted more than anything in the world. She was almost seven, long past time for a girl to have her own bicycle, but her daddy had told her the bicycle factories were too busy making tanks for the soldiers to fight the Germans. Cheap junk. That's all there was out there, cheap junk, and her daddy wasn't one for that. She'd just have to wait until the war was over, he said.

"I sure would, Ma'am, but there's nothing but junk in the stores," Birdi said.

"Maybe there's one that's not for sale," Mrs. Hamm said.

"I wouldn't know about that, Ma'am."

"Maybe there's a bicycle right now in the garage that's not junk," Mrs. Hamm said.

"Whose bicycle?"

"Maybe it's yours." Her voice sort of sang it.

Birdi was confused. "I don't think so," she said.

"Go on out there," Mrs. Hamm said. "If you find a bicycle in that garage, it belongs to you."

And there it stood near the door of the spotless garage, all by itself, clean and fresh, ready to go. It was painted black with cream-colored stripes, not red and shiny like the Schwinn she dreamed about. It was second-hand, she could tell, but the tires and steel handle bars looked new. It was a girl's bike; it was a Columbia; it was the most beautiful thing Birdi had ever seen.

When she went back upstairs to make sure this bicycle was really hers, the old lady was lying on her back, her mouth open, snoring. Birdi took hold of one of her velvety-soft old-lady hands and cradled it against her cheek.

"Thank you," she whispered. "I love it so much."

Mr. Hamm was Harris Reynolds' boss, the Hamm of Hamm Hardware, the Hamm of "If you're handy, go to Hamm." And Harris Reynolds was Birdi's daddy. He had worked for Hamm since high school and knew the business, top to bottom. No other hardware store had ever succeeded in Spotswood, a sleepy town of about forty thousand in southern Virginia, because Harris took care of Hamm's customers. The old man was an enigma to most of Spotswood. Silent and stiff-faced, his balding head bent slightly forward, his light blue eyes fixed on the papers before him, he shut himself up in the inner office most of the day, rarely looking up from the large book he scribbled in. Harris, on the other hand, bounced around the cluttered store, shaking hands, giving advice, demonstrating power tools, laughing, talking. He was a robust young man, a little heavy around the middle, with thick red-brown curls, large brown eyes, and the beginning of a double chin. The kind of young man people trusted.

Once a year, at Christmas, Hamm invited Harris and his family to a dinner of roast chicken, mashed potatoes, carrots and chocolate cake, all of which had been purchased in cardboard cartons from the Spotswood Hotel dining room. On these occasions, Mrs. Hamm left her bed and appeared downstairs in a navy blue silk dress and black and white spectator pumps.

Before they sat down to eat, Reva always played the Steinway piano which dominated the living room. She sat with a straight back on the piano bench, her light blue eyes, her father's eyes, fixed on the music stand, while her audience perched uncomfortably on faded Queen Anne chairs and a brown velveteen horsehair sofa. First there would be Christmas carols, then selections from Handel's *Messiah*, and always at the end a rousing rendition of the *Alleluia Chorus*. The first time Birdi was invited, she responded by contributing her thin four-year-old voice to the concert. But no one joined her, and no one smiled or looked in her direction except Mrs. Hamm, and so, midway through *Away in a Manger*, she stopped singing and never raised her voice again. Instead, she focused on Reva's heavy shoes pumping the pedals. Reva dressed for these occasions, like her mother, in a blue silk dress, but the fabric seemed softer, and the skirt swept low over her legs, almost hiding the shoes, but not quite. Her hands, thin and bony with prominent blue veins and long fingers, spread out along the keys, lifting, arching, crashing down.

After the concert, they filed into the dimly lit dining room which was barely large enough for the walnut table. Geneva, the maid, had to hold her breath as she squeezed herself between the guests and the dark green walls, serving the dinner with a weary smile. The center piece of plastic plums and bananas in a silver-plated bowl was an annual fixture; time had yellowed the lace cloth.

At the table, Mrs. Hamm sat herself next to Birdi and made sure she got plenty of mashed potatoes and chocolate cake.

It was after one of these dinners that Birdi began her visits to Mrs. Hamm's sick room. She was five at the time, and Mrs. Hamm told her she had lots of wonderful books she would like to read to her. And so the weekly visits began, with Mrs. Hamm sitting up in bed, a stack of books beside her, and Birdi on a stool close by.

"What's wrong with you?" she once asked.

"Nerves, dear," Mrs. Hamm said.

"Where do they hurt?"

"My head mostly."

"Do those pills make it feel better?"

"Most of the time."

"Will you read to me even after you get well?"

"I'll read to you forever if you like."

Birdi smiled at the old lady and scooted her stool even closer to the bed.

"Where'd that come from?" her daddy asked the day Birdi first rode the bicycle home.

"Mrs. Hamm gave it to me."

"For goodness sakes," her mother said.

"You sure she gave it to you? She didn't ask you to pay for it?" her daddy said.

"She didn't say anything about paying her. It's old. I think it was Reva's."

Mrs. Reynolds picked up the telephone right then and asked Mrs. Hamm about it.

"She's welcome to it, dear. No one's ridden it for years."

"Are you sure, Maddie? We'd be happy to pay you for it," Birdi's mother said.

"Don't be silly. You know I'd do anything for that child," was her reply.

The next day at the store, Harris told Hamm he thought he should pay for the bike.

"You'll have to ask the wife about that," Hamm said. "All I know is she asked me to clean it up. And I did."

Birdi was small for her age, with a sharply pointed nose and large black eyes. That's why they called her Birdi. Her real name was Roberta. Now that she had the Columbia, she took flight, racing around town, running errands for her mother, ringing the bell her daddy put on the handlebars, her thin brown hair streaming in wisps behind her, her skinny legs pumping.

She was riding down South Main under green-leafed maples one spring afternoon on the way home from school, when she nearly collided with a yellow rubber raincoat. Reva Hamm was inside the raincoat, crossing the street against a red light, and Birdi had almost hit her.

"Watch where you're going!" Reva's voice was harsh. But then she stopped and stared. "Oh it's you, Birdi," she said in the sort of polite tone adults use when talking to a child, and, smiling, she reached out and grabbed hold of the Columbia's handlebars.

Birdi was relieved. The harsh tone had startled her.

"Where'd you get your bicycle?" Reva asked.

"Your mama gave it to me."

Reva's smile was gone. "When was that?"

"Last month."

"Well, how 'bout that?" Reva said. She paused a minute, then said, "Are you sure?"

"Yes ma'am." Birdi was feeling uneasy.

Reva suddenly smiled and released her grip on the handlebars. "Well, you run along now and try to be more careful."

Birdi almost said, "Who wasn't being careful?" but instead she hopped on her bike and raced home.

The next morning, when Birdi's father opened the front door for his morning paper, he found Jerry Batson, a local policeman, standing on the front stoop.

"Morning, Harris," the policeman said. "I'm wondering if you got a Columbia bicycle anywhere around here?"

"Sure. It's Birdi's bike."

"Well, I'd like to take a look at it. We got a report of a stolen Columbia."

"Help yourself. But ours isn't stolen."

"Yeah? Hamm's daughter called it in."

"That's mighty peculiar, Jerry. Mrs. Hamm *gave* Birdi the bike."

The policeman raised his eyebrows. "Peculiar's the word for that girl all right. The mother too. But, I got orders to take possession. You can settle things with Hamm. Sorry about that, Harris."

Harris stood silent for a minute. "Look, Jerry," he finally said, "I myself offered to pay Hamm for that bike. How about you hold off until I talk to him?"

Birdi appeared from behind her daddy, peering up at the policeman with tears in her eyes.

"I guess that's OK," he said, looking down. "But I better not hear about it again."

As soon as the policeman was gone, Birdi raced to the garage and jumped on the bicycle seat, one foot on the cement floor, the other tucked around the black and cream frame. "It's mine," she pleaded, when her father approached. "Mrs. Hamm gave it to me."

"Maybe she meant to just lend it to you for a while," he said.

Her lower lip began to tremble. "She *gave* it to me."

"Okay. But I think we need to talk to her."

Birdi's mother came out from the house and put her hand on Birdi's head. "Let me do it," she said. "I know her better."

"You're right," Harris said. Birdi saw him look at her mother in a way she didn't understand.

"You're not taking my bike," Birdi said, winding her arms around the handlebars and pressing her cheek against the bell.

"All right," her mother said. "We'll both take it."

"No!" Birdi screamed.

Her mother pulled her off the bicycle with fingers stronger than they looked and wiped her face with a washcloth. "I'm sure there's a mistake, and we'll bring your bike back home. But the policeman says we have to make sure the bike's yours. I'm sorry, but that's how it is."

They headed together over to the Hamm's house. When they got to the front door, Birdi rested the Columbia on the kickstand, carefully locked it, and dropped the key deep in the pocket of her shorts. Geneva let them in.

"No company, Geneva." It was Mrs. Hamm's feeble voice, coming from upstairs.

"It's just me and Birdi," Ms. Reynolds called back. "We need to see you."

"Geneva, tell her to come back later." Something about Mrs. Hamm's voice struck Birdi as different, and she wanted to leave right then.

But Birdi's mother yelled out, "It won't take a minute, Maddie," and pulled the reluctant Birdi up the stairs behind her.

They found Mrs. Hamm in her bed as usual, her hands nervously twisting the blanket with the cornflower pattern; her gray hair hung loose around her colorless face, her watery blue eyes seemed puzzled. The room smelled funny to Birdi, slightly sweet and not pleasant.

Birdi's mother cleared her throat and announced in a loud voice, "Maddie, look at me."

Mrs. Hamm stared in the direction of the visitors.

"Maddie," Birdi's mother repeated. "Reva claims Birdi stole her bicycle."

Birdi stood very still beside her mother and looked at the floor. She knew something terrible was going to happen.

The old lady's eyelids fluttered.

"Why Birdi," she whispered, "I can't believe you'd do such a thing."

Birdi looked up, startled. "Do what?" Her face suddenly felt hot and she was crying. "I didn't steal anything. It's mine. You gave it to me."

"Really?" Mrs. Hamm frowned like she was trying to remember something that had happened a long time ago.

Birdi's mother looked closely at the old lady. "But I thanked you for it,

Maddie," she said. "On the telephone. And you said you'd do anything for my girl."

But Mrs. Hamm was no longer watching them. Her eyes had fixed on the door.

"Did you bring it back?" It was Reva, standing in the doorway, her limp brown hair pulled back from her face with bobbie pins, her light blue eyes shining out of dark hollows.

Mrs. Hamm reached out and gripped Birdi's arm with icy fingers but her eyes were still fixed on her daughter.

"Did I give Birdi your bike, dear?" she asked.

"Of course not," Reva spat out.

"We'll return the bicycle," Birdi's mother said. "Now." She was standing very stiff, and Birdi could tell by her voice she was angry.

"No," Birdi wailed. "It's my bike." She pulled her arm away from the old lady. "You gave it to me. It's mine."

But Mrs. Hamm wasn't listening. "Did you bring my medicine?" she said, her voice low, pleading.

"Yes, Mama." Reva grinned as she turned to Birdi. "Now then," she said. "Please go away. You're making her sick."

Without another word, Birdi's mother took hold of her daughter's hand and pulled her out of the room. Birdi fought her all the way down the stairs, but her mother's anger was stronger than her own.

Reva followed them out the front door.

"Where should we leave the bicycle?" Birdi's mother asked in a cold voice.

"No," Birdi screamed. "I won't."

"Just leave it here, by the front door." Reva looked at the bicycle. "It's locked. Where's the key?"

"You can't have it!" Birdi cried.

"You got no choice, honey," her mother said. "Hand it over."

Birdi threw the key at Reva and wrapped her arms around the Columbia's handlebars and kissed each one. Then carefully, lovingly, she leaned her bicycle back up against the kickstand and walked away. She held her mother's hand all the way home because she was crying too hard to see.

Early the next morning Harris Reynolds found the bicycle on his front stoop, its spokes bent and broken, the fender smashed, the tires flat.

"Keep Birdi inside," he whispered to his wife who was standing behind him, her hand over her mouth. But it was too late. Birdi pushed past both of them and threw herself onto the battered bicycle, pressing her hands against the busted wheels and crying out in jerky gasps. When her daddy tried to pick her up, the bicycle came with her. So he swooped them both up, laid them carefully in the back of his Dodge truck, and headed for the Hamms.

Hamm opened the door before Harris had even rung the bell. He was dressed, as usual, in his blue suit and starched white shirt, but his shoulders sagged and his usually sharp blue eyes were bloodshot.

"It's busted," Harris announced, thrusting the Columbia out in front of him. "How come?"

Hamm stared at the bicycle. He opened his mouth as if he were about to say something, but nothing came out.

They heard someone calling weakly from upstairs. "Who is it?"

"Never mind, dear," Hamm called back to her.

"It's Birdi, isn't it? Tell her to come up." The voice was soft, pleading.

Birdi stared up at Mr. Hamm. She was crying and her nose was running, unchecked.

"Birdi?" The voice from upstairs.

The child shook her head from side to side.

"Please, please, Birdi, come up."

Birdi turned back toward her wounded bicycle.

"I've got some new books," the voice promised.

But Birdi was crouched over her Columbia, caressing the fenders, kissing the pedals, her wet cheek resting on the seat.

"Birdi, come back. I miss you . . ." But the rest of whatever Mrs. Hamm was going to say was drowned out by a sudden crash of chords on the piano. Someone was playing a hymn, except it was too harsh, too loud, like one hand was banging fiercely on the piano while the other was picking out a tune.

Birdi peered around Hamm into the living room. Reva sat at the piano, smiling. Her eyes were focused on the sheet of music before her; her hands pounded the keys, her feet on the pedals were barefoot. And the big toe on her right foot was standing straight up.

GREEN SPRING VALLEY

<u>1936</u>

The white hair surprised him. The last time Pete was home, his father's thick, coarse hair had been brown. That was 1924, the year Pete married. But the broad shoulders stretching the seams of the blue serge suit, the thick fingers folded over the barrel chest, the shelf of brow over the closed eyes were just as he remembered. Pete knew he should cry, but he couldn't. Especially when he heard, for at least the third time, his brother's account of the old man's death.

"Luckily, I was visiting home when it happened." Preston's voice was deep, confident. "Houston came racing in the house, panting. 'Yo Pa,' he kept saying and pointed out toward the pasture. 'Fell in the creek.' I ran quick as lightning. Found him lying on his back under the willows, where Houston had pulled him out of the water. His coveralls were soaked, face gone white. When I took off my shirt to make a pillow for him, he felt stiff in my arms."

Always the same, Pete thought. Preston to the rescue.

"I asked him, 'Can you wiggle your fingers, Dad?' He just lay there, nothing moving but his lips. I put my ear next to his mouth, but all I could hear was him gulping for air. I knew right off he'd had a stroke. Next thing, he was shaking all over and making weird sounds, and his cheek next to mine was wet." Preston paused for effect. "He was crying."

"No!" Pete tried to stop him. His father didn't cry.

"It happens," Preston assured him. "I've seen it in my practice, time and again. You'd be surprised. Even the most stoic patients. I talked to him like he was a child, told him he was going to be okay. When I saw there was nothing more I could do, I put Houston in charge, and raced back to the house for my Ford. Drove hell for leather, bumping and bouncing over the fields to where I'd left him. His eyes were wide open, staring. I put my ear down on his chest. Like this." He leaned down to demonstrate. "Nothing. He was gone."

Pete waited for sadness to take him over or even anger at the old man lying in state in the family's dimly-lit front parlor. But all he felt was resentment toward his brother, Dr. Preston the expert, Dr. Preston the man in charge.

Later, as he was leaving the house for the funeral, he felt a tug on his sleeve. Preston's wife, Mary Lee, pulled him aside. "Pete, honey," she said, "I've saved up a big bag of Lee Ann's dresses. I thought your Kate might find some she likes."

"Thank you kindly, Mary Lee," he said. He felt his sister-in-law's soft hand as she handed him a valise.

"I'm just trying to help," she whispered.

When he looked up, Pete saw his brother standing at the front door, watching him, pity in his eyes.

"Don't," he said more harshly than he intended.

Later that night, after the funeral, after the crowd of church folks and neighbors had dropped off their casseroles and pies and left the house, Pete wandered back to the tiny kitchen where his mother was sitting at the table, her blue eyes magnified by the thick lenses of old age. As soon as he came in, she jumped up and wrapped her boney arms around him. Her cheek felt dry against his neck and she smelled like yeast bread.

"Thank you, sweet Pete," she whispered.

He smiled at the name she'd always called him. "For what, Mama?"

"Coming all this way. I know you don't have the money."

"I manage."

"How many years has it been?"

"Since . . . ?"

"Since we last saw you?"

"Let's see." He paused, trying to figure it out. He'd just gotten married. "Twelve years," he said.

"That long?"

"I brought Margaret down, remember?" He'd wanted to show her the farm.

His mother nodded.

He hesitated. "It didn't work out so good."

His mother turned away. "She was different. We didn't know how to take her."

"She was Catholic."

"I guess your father had trouble with that."

"He called her a Papist." He'd also told her a woman's place was in the home, when he knew full well she was clerking at the drug store. Pete recalled how that had rankled Margaret.

"He always spoke his mind."

Pete let that go. "How you doing, Mama?"

"I'm okay. Feel a little broken inside. Can't cry anymore. Tears got wrung out of me."

Pete pulled her into his arms. Her body was so small. The obvious thing to say was, you're tough, you'll get through it, which was true. But those words seemed hollow, predictable. So he said what he was feeling: "I love you."

She smiled up into his face. "I know."

He motioned her to follow him to the kitchen table.

"I wish I could do something," he said when they were seated, reaching across the table for her hand.

She squeezed his thick, farmer hand. "You know what you can do," she said.

He looked away. "I can't, Mama. You know that."

"What I know is, this place needs a farmer, now your father's gone."

He shook his head. "I can't move. I got a job and family where I live."

"You could all live here. There's plenty of room."

He sighed and stood up.

"Can't do it, Mama."

1918-1921

He was thirteen when it struck, the illness, and in the beginning, it seemed like the usual winter cold. All of them had suffered it, had complained of a sore throat, a fever. But Pete couldn't shake it. Preston and Mabel returned to school, but Pete's temperature kept climbing. Then his knees hurt and his shoulders, and the muscles in his legs ached so bad he couldn't walk. They all feared it was the flu, which in 1918 was in full swing and killing people. But when red bumps popped out on his chest, Dr. Bailey stopped calling it flu. By that time, Pete was too sick to understand what was happening to him. All he remembered was hurting all over in a dark room, people whispering, his mother sitting by his bed wiping him down with a wet cloth.

He found out later he'd come close to dying. It was rheumatic fever and there was no cure, no medicine. He just had to wait it out and hope his heart wouldn't be damaged. But his heart *was* damaged; two of the valves, he found out later, were in such bad shape they weren't much use. By the time he'd finally gotten well enough to make it back to school full-time, he was fifteen years old and had missed two years. He felt left behind, lonely. Preston, his younger brother who had always looked up to him, imitated him, adored him, was now in ninth grade, while Pete, a year older than his brother, was stuck with children half his size in the eighth.

"That stuff's easy," Preston would say when Pete sought his help with complex fractions. "Wait til you get to ninth and they give you algebra. Now *that's* hard." Or, "Are you coming to the gym tonight to watch me debate? The topic is *Should ROTC be required in high school.* I'm arguing against, which is pretty hard, don't you think? But Miss Naylor says I'm the best. So who knows?" And home he would come with his fake-gold trophy.

At sixteen Preston won a scholarship to the University, all expenses paid, while Pete failed geometry, bribed his younger sister Mabel to write his English reports, and increasingly found excuses to cut school. His father was not amused.

"What's the matter with you, boy? Gustafsons don't fail."

"I'm not cut out for school," Pete said.

"Well, you're not going to be cut out for anything if you don't buckle down and stop dawdling."

Pete's cheeks turned red. "I don't dawdle," he hissed. "I'm a good worker."

Rudolph Gustafson grabbed his son's shoulders with thick hands. "You look here, boy," he said. "I ain't talking milking cows. I'm talking studying."

"*You* milk cows," Pete shot back.

"Yeah. I didn't have the money for education," his father said. "But I've knocked myself out for you boys, and you are going to college. Just like your brother."

Pete pulled away, headed for the door.

"You come back here, boy," his father demanded.

But Pete slammed the front door and was gone—into the green Virginia hillsides that he loved.

Because once he had regained his strength, he loved nothing better than waking in summer at 4:00 a.m., watching the scarlet sky dissolve into blue, rushing into the valleys of velvet grass, milking the cows, washing the separator, driving the four-horse plow, picking tobacco, feeding the chickens and gathering their eggs, soaking up the early morning sun, falling dead asleep right after supper. Often he would feel winded or weary, but his shoulders had filled out, the muscles in his arms were long, powerful.

At seventeen, Pete stumbled on an article in *The Farm Journal* about dairy farming in Pennsylvania. It claimed that farmers were looking for men willing to work hard for good pay. He cut out the article and hid it under his pillow to read at night before blowing out the candle.

"I'm thinking of going up north to work," he told his mother.

Eva Gustafson nearly dropped the bucket of hot water she was carrying to the zinc tub in the kitchen for Pete's weekly bath. "What on earth gave you that idea?" she asked.

Pete bent, naked to the waist, over the side of the tub. "I'd like a change," he mumbled.

His mother dumped the hot water over his back. "What do you mean, change?"

He stood up, water dripping into his eyes, down his neck, and looked straight into his mother's face. "Papa doesn't want me to farm."

She looked away. Then, "How you going to get up north?"

Pete pulled a train schedule out of his damp back pocket. He had underlined the Southern Railway times table from Richmond to Philadelphia.

"Rudy!" his mother cried out. "Get in here. This boy's talking crazy."

When Rudolph Gustafson heard his son's plan, his large square face turned red. "You ain't going nowhere. You will stay right here, boy, and finish your education."

And he might have stayed. But he didn't. It was Christmas and Preston was home from the University, bragging about how his chemistry professor had called him a "prodigy."

"You need to buckle down, Pete," Preston told him. "You'll never get admitted to UVA unless you take your schoolwork more seriously."

This from his little brother. "You puffed up little weenie," Pete yelled and, without giving it a moment's thought, kicked Preston hard in the butt.

His brother whirled around, his cheeks red, and raced after Pete.

"Come on," Pete sang out. "Try to catch me." Suddenly, he pitched forward, stumbling and bouncing down the full flight of stairs from their bedroom, a staircase he had leaped easily, gracefully countless times before. But this time, his cheek caught on an exposed nail where a framed square of his mother's embroidery had recently been hanging. Blood streamed down his face as the full weight of Preston's body came crashing down on top of him.

Then blood was everywhere, on his shirt, in his hair, pooled on the floor. He remembered the drive in the buggy, his father at the reins, his cheek smarting underneath the towel his mother had pressed against the open cut. Preston sitting next to him, apologizing, crying.

The day after the stitches came out, Pete snuck out of the house before anyone was awake, walked in the freezing January chill the eight miles to the Spotswood bus station, paid for his ticket to Richmond with money he'd saved selling eggs, and vanished.

1936

Back in Pennsylvania after the funeral, Pete stumbled into the front door, threw down his carpet bag, and nearly collapsed into Margaret as she rushed to meet him.

"Oh sweet Jesus, I knew you shouldn't go." His wife wrapped her thick arms around him, half holding him up.

Pete leaned into her, giving himself up to her softness, her kitchen smell of tomatoes and onion, her broad hands on his back. When he had recovered his breath from the two flights of stairs, he smiled. "I'm fine, Peg. Really. I'm okay."

"Well you look like shit," she said as she maneuvered him over to the faded loveseat, a hand-me-down from Pete's boss. "What did they do to you down there?"

He laughed. "Killed me with kindness."

"So you told them?"

"Why would I do that?"

"They need to know."

"I don't go begging to my family," he said.

"I'm not asking you to beg. But Preston's a doctor."

"What can he do? My valves are done for."

"He might know something our doctor doesn't."

"The arrogant son of a bitch." Pete spat it out. "I'm fine. Really. I just need some loving and a good night's sleep."

"Well I love you," she said. "Good thing you're not too proud to ask for that."

He woke up the next morning with eight-year-old Kate balancing a cup of hot tea over him.

"Good God. What time is it?" He threw off the quilt and looked around. Compared to his childhood bedroom in Green Spring Valley, the small, dimly lit room felt cramped. The bulky oak wardrobe he'd picked up in an auction took up most of one wall and Kate's bed was shoved up against the wall opposite, leaving very little space on the wood floor for maneuvering. His ten-year-old son Rudy slept in the kitchen, on a mattress they rolled up during the day.

"Stay where you are, Daddy," his daughter said, pulling back the curtains from the one narrow window, which looked out on a brick apartment building. "Mama says you got to stay in bed a day or two. I'm to look after you."

"Where's Rudy?"

"At school."

"What about you?"

She grinned. "Rudy reported me sick."

Pete smiled at his bone thin daughter, his treasure, as she eased herself up on the bed beside him. "I don't like you missing school, Honey."

"Mama wanted you shouldn't be alone," she said. "Besides, just this once won't matter. They're repeating stuff I already know."

He hugged her and laughed. "Smarty-pants," he said and pointed to the corner. "See that valise over there? Your Aunt Mary Lee sent you some clothes."

"Uh-oh."

"Why don't you look? You might be surprised."

Kate bounced out of bed and started yanking one dress after another from the valise.

"Look a here!" She held up a stiff pink organdy with a satin sash hanging off it.

She pulled her homemade cotton dress over her head and wriggled into her cousin's hand-me-down. Her thin arms poked out of the puffed sleeves and the skirt brushed her ankles.

"Let's have a look at you," Pete said, and he and Kate both burst out laughing.

"I'm a princess," she giggled, prancing around the room, her thin brown pigtails bouncing, one tie of the pink sash wrapped around her scrawny neck, the other trailing the floor.

"There must be some school clothes in there," Pete said.

Kate held up a soft cotton print with elaborate smocking from collar to waist.

"It's pretty, don't you think?" Pete asked.

Kate tossed it back toward the valise. "Yeah." Her voice was almost wistful. "But I'd get laughed out of class if I came marching into school with that smocked-up thing."

"Put 'em back," Pete said. "Your mother will find some use for them." Which meant they would be sold to a second-hand shop in Philadelphia for money the family badly needed.

1921-1936

Pete had found a good job when he first came to Pennsylvania, working a dairy farm for Ross Jennings, a gentleman farmer who sat in the State Legislature. Pete loved farming, loved the vast green hills, the roomy barn with its clean stalls and freshly cut hay, the small tenant cabin his Margaret kept spotless. His beautiful young bride. Rich, that's the word that came to him when he buried himself in all her softness, when he loosened her dark, thick hair from the untidy pile on her head and breathed its sweetness. His Margaret had none of the false modesty of the girls he'd grown up with, but looked him square in the face, inviting him to pay attention, insisting with her eyes that he touch her, love her. And he did. She was part of the enchanted playground he had stumbled upon and which his two babies had rolled around in. His Papa had been wrong. Learning to farm back in Virginia was all the education he'd ever want or need.

When the family outgrew the one room cabin Mr. Jennings made available, they moved to the rented apartment in Greenwood, the town closest to the farm. Three dark rooms, parlor, kitchen, bedroom, on the top floor of a three-story building. A patch of grass out back with a sandbox. To help with the rent, Margaret went back to her old job clerking at Johnson's Drugs.

When the first attack came, it didn't stop him. He'd had a pain in his chest for months, which he'd ignored. Then a fever laid him low for a couple of weeks. The local doctor sent him to Philadelphia for tests, which confirmed myocarditis.

"Your heart's working overtime," Dr. Reynolds said. "Try to take it easy for a while."

"How'm I supposed to do that, doc?" he asked. "I got mouths to feed."

"Get yourself a desk job."

Pete laughed. As soon as he was on his feet, he was back to working fourteen hour days, waking before light, milking, feeding, binding, plowing with the new John Deere, carrying cold biscuits in his pocket for when he got hungry, mending fences, striding the green fields.

As the years went by, there were relapses and high fevers and pain and days in bed, then weeks.

1940

Then one winter afternoon, four years after Pete's father's funeral, Mr. Jennings came to the apartment carrying a sack of Florida grapefruit.

"I hate like stink to do this, Pete," his boss said. "You're the best manager I ever met. But fact is, I need somebody full time, every day. And you need to take care of your health."

Pete protested, claimed he was getting better all the time, but he knew Mr. Jennings was right.

"I'm not firing you, Pete; don't get that idea. You're indispensable on this farm. But you'll be working alongside the new man."

"Sounds like an hourly wage."

"I'm afraid so."

At thirty-six, Pete still worked on the farm when he was well, and Margaret took in sewing on the weekends. And for a while, things were good again.

For one thing, Pete now had more time with his children. His own father had paid little attention to him growing up. So his notion of being a father was to work fourteen hours a day and pay the bills. But now he had time to play catch with his son, to take long walks into the countryside with Kate, picking wild flowers and looking their names up afterwards in a book he found at the county library, all the while marveling at the sharp wits of his offspring, their innate sweetness.

At fourteen, Rudy was already taller than his father. He imitated Pete's long-legged stride as he crossed the meadows rounding up Mr. Jennings' stray cows, milking them with strong, sure fingers, talking soft to the horses like his dad. And Rudy was clever with his hands, turning spare boards into kitchen shelves for his mother, fashioning a boat he often sailed on the small lake near Greenwood.

But it was Kate who brought Pete to life when he was stuck in the house, too ill to work. She spent hours on the floor of his bedroom, cutting printed models out of her mother's pattern magazines. Prancing them about the bedroom, acting out scenes from her vivid imagination.

"Why's that lady up on the wardrobe?" Pete would ask.

"She's learned how to fly. And they all hate her, because she won't tell them how."

"Why doesn't she?"

"They won't let her play with them."

"Why not?"

Whisper. "They think she might be a witch."

"Is she?"

"I haven't decided."

When Pete could no longer count on being well enough to farm, Margaret got a job as a receptionist in the local dentist's office. The pay was better than the drug store job, which she still worked on Saturdays. But many bills went unpaid.

At a knock on the door, Pete struggled to sit up.

"Who is it?" he yelled.

A voice called back, but he couldn't hear the name.

More knocking.

"Hold on," Pete called out. "I'm coming."

He pulled himself up, reached for his trousers which were draped over the iron frame at the foot of the bed, and fumbled his way into them. Forcing himself to walk one step at a time, he reached the door.

The brothers stared at each other.

"My God," Preston burst out.

Pete stood in the doorframe, unshaven, his thin hair sticking up at angles, his undershirt stained, his pants unzipped, and he laughed. Because the man facing him, his brother, in his navy-blue suit, perfectly molded to his frame, a suitcase in one hand, a doctor's bag in the other, had the same sandy-colored hair, parted in the middle, the same piercing brown eyes, the same shelf of a brow as he did.

"Well, Preston," he said. "You've got a tailor, a good barber, and a lot of money. But all the same you're an ugly Gustafson, just like me."

Suddenly Pete's knees crumpled under him. Preston dropped both bags, grabbed his brother around the waist, and half holding him, half carrying him, walked him back into the bedroom and stretched him out on the bed.

"Is this what you came for?" Pete asked, staring up at the brother he hadn't seen for four years, not since the funeral.

"We need to get you to a hospital."

"I've been. I'm not going back."

Preston sat down on the bed next to Pete. "You need meds," he said. "The nurses can make you comfortable, keep you hydrated. Watch over you."

Pete smiled. "I've got . . ."

"Margaret. I know. Where is she?"

"At work."

"You can't give up, Petey." Preston's voice sounded urgent. "You're only thirty-six, for god's sake."

"*Petey?*" Pete raised himself up on his elbows and looked hard at his brother. "Why the hell are you here?"

"I came to find out how you are."

"Now you see." Pete collapsed back on the bed. "Come on, tell me what's going on."

Preston shrugged his way out of his suit coat, folded it carefully over the railing at the end of the bed, then settled himself on a metal chair he had dragged from the kitchen.

"At Dad's funeral," he finally said, "you acted like, I don't know, like I'd done something wrong." He sat for a minute, staring into space, avoiding Pete's eyes. "Like you almost hated me."

So they were going to have a real conversation. Pete felt a burst of his old energy and spit it out. "Aside from the fact that you're rich as hell and I'm dirt poor, that you got the stamp of approval from the old man and I was a failure? That you haven't even visited me in all the time I've lived up here? Aside from that, why am I angry?" Pete's outburst brought on a coughing fit so violent that for a minute he couldn't catch his breath.

Preston rushed to the kitchen for a glass of water and held it to his brother's mouth.

Pete took a sip, then whispered, "Please leave."

"I can't. You're way too ill. I may be a lousy brother, but I'm a good doctor."

"I don't want your help. I don't want your money. I don't want . . ." Pete reached for the glass, took a swallow ". . . your kids' cast offs."

Preston seemed to shrink into himself. "We were close, Pete, when we were kids." His voice was soft. "What happened?"

"You know as well as I do."

"I only know you were my big brother. I looked up to you, wanted to be like you. And then you got sick, and after that you turned on me."

Pete laughed. "That's just like you -- blaming me." He fixed his eyes on Preston. "Don't you remember? You lorded it over me, bragging about how you skipped two grades."

"That was Dad who did the bragging."

"No, Preston, it was you."

"What I remember is trying to help you with your homework."

"How do you think that made me feel?"

"You didn't like it. But I wanted you back. You'd been sick so long."

"You're rewriting history, brother."

"Maybe. But it's how I remember it."

Pete pulled himself up to a sitting position. "You pushed me down the stairs. Remember? And I cut my face wide open."

Preston stared. "That was a fight. We were kids. You got mad and kicked me and I ran after you. I didn't push you. You jumped. Come on, Pete. You were always jumping down those stairs; only that time you stumbled."

"I was covered in blood. And you were on top of me."

"I tripped and fell down the stairs behind you."

"That's your story."

Preston shook his head. "I don't believe you're still angry because of one fight."

"It's not that." Pete lay back on the pillow. He was so tired.

"What then?"

"You've always been the brainy one," Pete said, his voice fading. He hated bringing up all this past history.

"Even if it's true, is that a reason to hate me?"

"At least I was bigger and stronger, better at ball games." It was as if Pete were talking to himself. "After I got sick . . . you bragged . . . left me behind . . . I was nothing."

"You had Mama," Preston said.

Pete looked up, surprised. "What's that supposed to mean?"

"There wasn't much love in that house. Dad pushed us to achieve. But did you notice? He never hugged us, never even touched us. You had Mama."

"And you didn't?"

"Not really. I saw it happen when you got so sick. It was after nursing you for so long, fearing you wouldn't make it, that she came to favor you over me and Mabel. We both felt it." Preston reached over and took Pete's cold hand in his.

Pete shook him off.

Preston turned toward the window. "She wants you to come home," he said. "So do I. There's room for all of you in our old house." He looked around the crowded room. "A lot more room than here. And I can look after you."

"She already asked. At Dad's funeral. I said no then. Nothing's changed."

"That was four years ago. What's changed is you're too sick to work."

"You come up here for the first time ever and ask me to give up . . ."

"You're sick, Pete. And you can't support your family."

"Get out!"

"No. Blame me as much as you want. Blame the old man. But it's not our fault you're too sick to work. I can get you on your feet again."

"Too late."

"It's your Green Spring Valley, Pete. You know you love it. Once you're on your feet, you can farm again. Margaret can get a job in my office at twice what's she's making here. The kids can have all that fresh air, all those green fields, horses."

He's rehearsed that speech, Pete thought, but all the same his mind flooded with green, grass green, deep blue-green, yellow spring green, maple and dogwood spread over hills, over pastures. He could almost smell the sting of wild onion, the sweet scent of apple blossoms.

Suddenly there was Margaret. At the bedroom door, her navy straw hat plunked down to her ears, her eyebrows raised in question. Rudy and Kate just visible behind her. He smiled. "This is home," he mumbled.

"How do you do?" Margaret walked briskly into the room and faced Preston.

"Margaret," he said, shaking her hand. "It's been too long."

"Sixteen years," she said in a matter of fact voice. "Rudy, Kate, come here and meet your Uncle Preston."

Rudy solemnly offered his hand to his uncle.

Kate peered up at him. "You're Uncle Preston? I didn't expect you to look so much like my dad." She stood, patient, stiff, as Preston reached out in a clumsy attempt to hug her.

"Now then, out of here," Margaret said, pointing to the door. "Time for this man to get some rest." And planting a kiss on her husband's mouth, she led them all to the kitchen.

It had already turned dark, when Pete jolted awake, surprised to find someone's hand resting on his. Preston was sitting on the chair beside his bed, watching him.

"Did you manage to sell her?" Pete asked, pulling his hand away.

"I tried."

"And?"

"She'll do what you want."

"I told you my answer."

"Just be sure you aren't turning this down because I'm the one who offered it."

"Mama did too."

"Come on Petey, aren't you just a little tempted by the Valley?

He was. Not just a little.

"Look, don't just dismiss the idea. Give it . . . ."

Pete cut him off. "You staying here tonight?" he asked.

Preston smiled. "I'm a little long for that loveseat in there. I've got a room at the hotel in town. Then off tomorrow to an office full of patients."

"I'm now supposed to say thanks for coming?"

"Not if you don't mean it."

Pete struggled to sit up. "Maybe I do. Some things need to be said."

Preston cupped his brother's shoulders in his hands and eased him back down on the bed. They watched each other in silence for several minutes.

Preston said, "They love you very much. I envy you."

Pete felt his brother touch his arm. He wanted to say something, but he was afraid of the tears he felt building up. So, he grabbed Preston's strong hand instead.

But then he stopped cold, stared at his brother, then hurled the dollar bills in the air. They landed on the sheet, on the floor, on the wardrobe, in Preston's face.

"Get out!" he shouted.

In bed that night, Pete put his arm around his wife's thick shoulders, buried his head in her neck and whispered.

"Well?"

"It's your decision."

He knew her so well. "Which means you think I'm a fool not to go."

"Why'd you ask if you know what I think?"

"I can't," he whispered. "Maybe I should, but I can't"

"I figured."

"You're not going to try to persuade me?"

"No," she said.

"You know what it means."

"Yep. And I hate it."

"And it's still up to me?"

"Yes," she said and pulled him tight against her.

He lay there long afterwards, eyes open, wide awake. He could barely make out the rounded lump of his Kate, huddled under the quilt, sleeping soundly. He tried not to think about what would happen when . . . She'd be fine. The children were tough.

But he couldn't get back to sleep.

GOING UNDER

You see, I really loved her. Not like the others. All the guys who *told* her they loved her. When all they really cared about was taking advantage.

Her name was Brenda. Brenda Hill. She came to our town last summer, right before we started eighth grade. The summer of 1954. The summer I decided to take Jesus as my personal savior and be baptized at First Baptist.

That day I was picking up my stack of papers for my afternoon route in front of the Langston Apartments, the way I always did, and there she was, out front on the concrete steps.

"Hi there, paperboy," she said. It was sticky hot, and she had on white shorts and a pink checked halter top, and she was barefoot. Her brown hair was short and brushed back in what they call a duck tail. And her eyes were deep black-brown.

"Hi," I said. "I'm Gordon. Are you new here or just visiting?"

"Moved in yesterday," she said. "And I'm about to melt."

Her face and shoulders were sunburned, not tanned brown like the rest of us, so I figured she was new to the southern weather.

"Where you from?" I asked.

"All over," she said. "We move a lot."

I liked her from the first. She was friendly and pretty and we had some nice talks. She was usually sitting on the steps when I came by to pick up my papers, and I would sit down beside her to roll them. Then she'd help me load up my bike basket with the rolled up newspapers. That's how I've been saving for college. They pay me to ride my bicycle through town and throw newspapers onto the front porches without having to stop. It's good money.

Brenda told me she had lived in Washington D.C. and Florida and even California. Her dad was retired military. And her mama was a secretary.

She started bringing me a glass of lemonade every afternoon, and I'd tell her about the teachers at school and who the nice kids were and the ones she should avoid. I told her about Reverend Coleman at our Church, how he was somebody you could talk to and he'd listen. I was too shy to ask her for a date. I was too shy to ask anybody for a date. I just liked her, liked talking to her, and looking at her, she was so pretty.

I didn't see much of her after school started that fall. She showed up now and then on the steps to chat, but I had to wait until after football practice to deliver my papers, and it was too cold by that time for sitting around.

Then one afternoon after practice, Joey Whitehead, a ninth grader and the j. v. quarterback, started talking about how that new girl, Brenda, was a hot ticket. He said he'd taken to going to her apartment after practice, and her mama worked, so she wasn't home. They'd drink lemonade or something first and pretend to do homework. Then they'd start French kissing.

"No shit!" Bobby Stokes said.

"Scout's honor," Joey said. "She starts it. She drops her pencil or something and slides over close to me to pick it up. Then she takes off my glasses and tells me she likes my blue eyes. I get the message she wants something, right? So I lean forward and put my hand on her tit. You know."

We didn't, but we wanted to.

Joey held back a minute, pulling us in. "Aw, I shouldn't tell you this stuff. She wouldn't like it."

So we begged.

"You get a hard on?" Bobby asked.

Joey laughed. "How else do you think I get it in, dickhead?"

"I don't believe you," I said. I thought of Brenda and how pretty she was and how much I liked her.

"You're such a kid, Gordy," he said, "She loves it."

"Where's her dad?" I asked.

"I never saw any dad," Joey said. "I don't think she has one."

"She does," I said, but nobody listened.

After that I'd see them together, in the halls at school or after the games. I'd see her rushing onto the field with everybody else. Joey would be all sweaty and his uniform would be muddy, and he'd put his arm around her shoulder and walk off the field, waving at his friends like some hero. And she'd be looking up at him and laughing. I wanted to kill him.

No, I wanted to tell her what kind of things he was saying about her. All the lies and bragging. But I didn't get a chance, because Joey's mama put an end to it. Somehow she got wind of what Joey was up to and started making him come right home after practice. I still didn't believe him, but then other guys, Bobby Stokes and Billy James and others, guys whose mothers didn't go to First Baptist like the rest of us, started talking.

"You going up to Brenda's today?" one of them would say.

"Nah. It's your turn." And they'd laugh.

Bobby would look at me and say, "How 'bout it, Gordy? All you have to do is tell her you love her. And then watch out for your braces."

I hated him.

But it started me thinking. I'd never kissed a girl, never even had a girlfriend. Maybe Brenda was the place to start. She was the only girl I'd ever felt comfortable just talking with. I thought I might tell her what the guys were saying and promise to set the story straight. But if she was the kind of girl they said, maybe she would kiss me too.

So I worked up my courage and the next time I picked up my papers at the Langston, I rang the doorbell of her apartment. After a long time she opened the door. She was wearing a blue terrycloth bathrobe.

She took one look at the stack of papers in my arms and said, "Oh. It's you."

"Who'd you think it was?"

"Nobody. Never mind. Want to come in?"

I'd never been inside her apartment before, and I was surprised at how empty it was. There was furniture, of course, a sort of saggy brown sofa and a couple of chairs. A TV. But there were no pictures on the walls and no lamps or rugs or figurines. Just a bare wood floor and a ceiling light.

She walked over to the sofa, sat down, and patted the cushion next to her. I pretended not to notice that the belt on her robe had come untied and I could see her leg all the way up to her underpants.

I sat down next to her, my bundle of papers in my lap. "Were you expecting Bobby Stokes?" I asked.

She laughed. "Maybe. It's OK. I'm glad to see you. It's been awhile." She nodded toward my papers. "Look, you want help with those?"

"Sure," I said and handed her a stack.

We sat rolling papers while I worked up my courage. "Look," I finally said, "I don't want to upset you, but I thought you should know. Bobby's been spreading lies about you."

She sat up real straight and pulled her robe around her. "What'd he say?"

I took a deep breath and blurted out. "He says if he comes here and tells you he loves you, you'll . . ." I couldn't say the words, "let him do things."

The silence was awful. She just kept staring at the rolled up papers. Finally she said, real low, "Do you believe him?"

"I said it was lies."

She turned toward me. She looked so good, sitting there like that, in her blue bathrobe, her brown eyes so dark and wet looking.

"You're really pretty," I said. I didn't know it was coming; it just popped out.

"You think I'm going to let you do things now?" she asked, laughing a kind of nasty laugh.

I felt my cheeks getting hot. "No. I'm sorry. I didn't mean it like that."

"How *did* you mean it?" She looked suspicious.

"I don't know," I mumbled. "I just mean you're pretty."

"Wait a minute," she said and got up and left the room. I sat there for about ten minutes, wanting to leave, not wanting to leave.

When she came back, she was wearing a blue and black plaid skirt and a red sweater, white socks and brown loafers. Her school clothes. She sat down on the sofa facing me and put her hands on either side of my face. I could feel her soft fingers on my cheeks; she smelled good, like Ivory soap. I wanted to kiss her, to touch her. I'd never felt this way before.

It looked like she'd been crying. At least her eyes were red. I didn't know what to say, so I just sat there hoping she wouldn't move her hands.

She looked right into my eyes and said, "Will you do something for me?"

"Sure." I didn't care what it was, I'd do it.

"Promise?"

"Of course."

"Okay," she said, "I want you to take me to that church of yours."

Just then the door burst open and this short, stocky man walked in. He had on a blue business suit, like my dad wears, but I thought he could use a haircut. He smiled at Brenda. She looked down at her lap and she wasn't smiling.

"Well, who is this?" he asked, nodding his head in my direction.

"It's Gordy," she said. "A friend."

"Nice to meet you, Gordy," he said and reached out to shake my hand. His was softer than I expected and I noticed his fingernails needed clipping. But he seemed pretty nice.

"I like this one," he said.

I looked over at her. But she just sat there, which I couldn't figure out, because her dad was watching her like he was waiting for her to say something.

"I better go," I said.

"Yeah," the man said, "You better go. It's getting late."

As I was heading out, Brenda suddenly looked up and said, "Remember what you promised." Her voice was cool, like it didn't really matter what she said. But her eyes looked different. She was begging me.

So that's how she started coming to First Baptist. In the beginning Mother was against it.

"How come she wants to go with us?" she asked. "Where's her family?"

"I guess they don't go to church."

"Well, I don't think much of that," she said.

"Look," I said, "Jesus welcomes everybody. Reverend Coleman is always saying that."

"Yeah, but I've heard rumors about that girl."

"Maybe she wants to change."

"Maybe she's after you."

I could only hope.

The next Sunday morning we found her waiting on the steps in front of the Langston Apartments. She had on a blue wool coat I hadn't seen before and a little rose-colored hat with a veil and white gloves. She thanked Mother for picking her up and sat in the back seat, real still, all the way to church.

First Baptist is the biggest church in Spotswood. Of course, like any town, there are Methodist and Presbyterian churches, but they're pretty small. Most people go to First Baptist, and that's because of Reverend Coleman. He's a big man, real tall, and he says complicated things in a simple way you can understand. You can tell him anything, and he says no matter how bad it is, Jesus will forgive you if you are truly repentant. We all sit there every Sunday in this big sanctuary, with flowers on the altar, the sun shining through the stained glass window of Jesus with the lambs, and we just feel good. I know church is boring for most people, but First Baptist is different.

The first time Brenda came, everyone was staring, trying to figure out what she was doing there, especially with me. But she paid no attention and just smiled and sang the hymns and bowed her head when we prayed. So after a while folks stopped staring.

Meanwhile, back at school, Bobby Stokes and his buddies complained.

"Brenda's got religion. She's no fun," they'd say.

Bobby claimed he still went to her place after school and messed around, but I knew he was lying, because I was there. After I delivered my papers every afternoon, I'd ring her doorbell. She always met me dressed in her school clothes. I never saw that blue bathrobe again. We'd do our homework or play Monopoly or just talk. I told her about my mama, how she had to work as a nurse since my dad died. She liked hearing about her. But when I asked her questions about her mother, she just said she was a secretary and then changed the subject.

The first time she let me kiss her, I got all dizzy and didn't know where to put my hands. All I could think was how soft her mouth was. How much I loved her. But that was it. If I tried anything funny, like putting my hand on her chest, she'd push me away.

So I held back. I tried to tell her how I felt about her several times, but she told me to hush, she didn't want to hear it. So I held it inside.

I always tried to leave before her mama and dad came home, but every once in a while her dad would show up.

"Hi kid," he'd say and mess up my hair or give me a mock punch in the chest. "How's Brenda getting on at First Church?"

"She's doing great, sir," I'd say, feeling confused. There was something about him that seemed to be making fun. But he was friendly enough and he was awfully fond of Brenda.

"How's my girl?" he'd say.

I always packed up my books when he showed up, and left.

I never saw her mama. Not once.

As I said, I had made the decision to take Jesus as my personal savior and join the church the summer I met Brenda. The time for my baptism had now come. It wasn't actually such a big decision. Everybody in our town joined the church when they were about my age, fourteen. But Reverend Coleman didn't just let you join up; he made sure you understood the step you were taking. There were Bible study classes you had to attend on Friday afternoons, and you had to have a private conference with Reverend Coleman. Finally, there was the baptism, total immersion.

On the first Friday of Bible study, I rang Brenda's doorbell after I'd delivered my papers to tell her I couldn't see her that day. But when she opened the door, she had her coat on.

"I'm going too," she said. "I'm joining the church."

"Are you sure?" I asked. "You've only been going about a month. Most people take longer than that."

"I want to be really saved," she said. "I want Reverend Coleman to wash away all my sins forever."

So, every Friday afternoon for the next two months, we met in a Sunday School classroom with about ten other kids to prepare to take Jesus as our savior. We learned about twenty Psalms by heart and played this game where you would open the Bible at any place and read the scripture out loud and try to figure out what it meant. Brenda was a whiz. She memorized the Bible passages faster than anybody else in the class, and she never goofed off.

On the last afternoon of Bible Study, Reverend Coleman asked us to come back to the church that night so that he could meet with each one of us separately. He said he was going to ask us about our lives and why we were making this decision. He talked about the seriousness of the step we were taking and how proud he was of all of us for choosing the Christian path and how he expected us to hold fast to our faith. He said the Baptism would take place on Sunday night. Then he gave everybody a Bible with a red leather cover.

I walked Brenda home as usual that Friday afternoon. It was March, the beginning of spring, and you could smell apple blossoms and the air was warm and sweet.

"How come you're so quiet?" I asked her.

She looked down and muttered something under her breath.

"What's that?"

She still didn't look at me, but I heard her this time. "I'm afraid," was what she whispered.

Now that surprised me. She'd never struck me as scared of anything. Certainly not a pool of waist-high water.

I'd seen dozens of baptisms and had studied the way it was done. We don't go to a river to be baptized in our church, like the primitive Baptists out in the country. We have a baptismal font right at the front of the sanctuary about the size of a bathtub, only deeper. They do the baptisms on Sunday nights after the sermon. Reverend Coleman and all the people being baptized wear choir robes over their underwear. But Reverend Coleman also wears hip-high rubber boots under his choir robe; he showed them to me once.

"Look, Brenda," I said. "There's nothing to be afraid of. When it's your turn, Reverend Coleman will take your hand and lead you down the stairs into the water. Which is warm, like in a bathtub. He'll take both your hands in his and say, 'I baptize thee, Brenda Hill, in the name of the Father, the Son, and the Holy Ghost,' then he'll put his hand over your face. You're supposed to hold your nose with your fingers, which are under his, and he'll tip you back into the water until it covers you. He'll bring you right back up and say to the congregation, 'Lord, it has been done as Thou hast commanded and yet there is room.' That's it."

"I'm talking about tonight."

"Tonight?" It made no sense. "We're just talking to Reverend Coleman tonight. You're surely not afraid of him?"

"Suppose you're too full of sin even for him," she said.

"That's why you get baptized," I said. "To wash your sins away."

"Suppose they won't wash."

"But they will. That's the whole point. You'll feel better after you talk to the Reverend tonight."

She smiled then. "Promise?"

"Promise." I kissed her then, on the lips, and she kissed me back.

That night I went by her apartment. I waited a long time, and finally Brenda's dad opened the door. He was in his undershirt, and I realized it was the first time I'd ever seen him without the blue suit.

"What do you want?" he asked.

"I came for Brenda."

He smiled this strange kind of smile. "She's not going."

"But the conferences with Reverend Coleman start in about fifteen minutes."

"I heard," he said.

And then I saw her. She was standing behind him in the dark living room.

"I'm sorry," she said. Her voice sounded strange. "I can't."

"Why?" I asked, peering around Mr. Hill to get a better look.

"She's not going," he repeated and shut the door in my face.

She didn't show up on Sunday night for the Baptism either. I was so sick at heart I could hardly pay attention. I do remember the water being colder than I expected. I kept trying to concentrate on Jesus, but I couldn't stop shivering and all I could think about was Brenda.

The next day at school she acted like she was avoiding me. So I waited by her locker after school.

"What happened?" I asked when she finally showed up.

"I told you before."

"You said you were afraid. But there wasn't anything to be afraid of."

"You don't get it."

"You would have been fine. Reverend Coleman would have held you up the whole time."

"Nobody's strong enough for that," she said. "Not even Reverend Coleman."

"What do you mean?"

She looked away. "Gordy," she said, "you have no idea."

That afternoon, when I rang her doorbell, nobody answered. I even thought I heard voices inside, so I banged on the door and called out to her. But nobody came.

A week later, when I went to pick up my papers, there was a moving van out front.

I went into the building. Brenda's front door was wide open, and the living room was a mess. Trash all over the floor, crumpled up paper, dust balls. Packing boxes. No furniture. I was about to leave when I saw something red sticking out of a pile of trash. I dug out Brenda's Bible and stuffed it in my jacket pocket.

I managed not to cry then, but that night at home, in bed, I cried. And that wasn't the only time. I kept seeing that room. Something had happened in there, something I couldn't understand.

The next Sunday I stuck around after church, then followed Reverend Coleman into his office. As soon as he shut the door, I burst out, "Brenda's gone. Her house is a wreck, she didn't say goodbye, she threw away her Bible, the one you gave her. She threw it in the trash." I was trying not to cry.

He motioned to the brown sofa and sat down beside me. It was quiet in there and it smelled really sweet from the flowers somebody had brought in. I handed him the red bible.

He flipped through the pages like he was looking for something. "You're worried about your friend," he said.

I nodded.

"Looks like she's moved," he said. "There's probably a good reason for it. I'm sure she's fine."

He didn't get it. "But she didn't get baptized," I said, "she stopped going to church."

"I know," he said. "I was disappointed about that. But maybe she wasn't ready. When she is, Jesus will welcome her and rejoice. You mustn't worry."

But I *was* worried and confused. I needed him to understand. I needed it really bad. "She told me she was too full of sin to be baptized."

"No one is too full of sin for God to forgive them," Reverend Coleman said. The same words, the same calm voice I'd heard so many times. But this time it didn't help.

Because all I could think about was Brenda and how scared she was. And how she had tried so hard and we hadn't been able to save her.

FASTER THAN A ROLLER COASTER

He's perched on that red armchair, as usual. My Pierce. Surrounded by bird nests. Mud and twigs. Leaves and bark. Some are hanging from hooks in the ceiling, like purses. Orioles. And there are tidy little cups. Goldfinch, I think. He's labeled some of the nests, the ones in glass cabinets; others are displayed on open shelves or falling apart on the scratched mahogany table his mother gave us.

"It's after midnight," I say.

He smiles up at me. I love his white hair. Premature at forty-two. I love his face, unlined, pale, boyish.

"I need an owl," he says.

"Pay attention, Pierce. She's sixteen and it's after midnight."

But there she is, my Clare, racing up the hall toward us, her red hair half out of her ponytail, bursting into the room we call The Museum, where Pierce keeps his collections.

"I'm sorry." She's panting. "We went for ice cream."

"That's no excuse."

"I said I was sorry." She brushes past me and wraps her arms around Pierce's neck. "Wayne wants to meet you, Daddy," she says. "I told him you play the clarinet. He plays piano, plays for parties and stuff."

"What kind of piano?" Pierce asks.

"Jazz," Clare says. "And dancing music, like Elvis and Buddy Holly."

"Concentrate, Pierce," I beg. "She's sixteen years old, coming in after midnight."

He pauses, looking up at me like he hears me. Then, "I *really* need a Great Horned nest."

Clare giggles. A late night, giddy sort of laugh.

I give up. I love her. And she's home.

The first time it happened, I was just her age, a high school majorette from the wrong side of the tracks. And he was a short skinny boy in the band, with hair so blond it was almost white and skin so pale he looked anemic. I could feel his eyes on me as I twirled my baton; he was marching along behind, tootling away on his clarinet.

And then one day he just disappeared; he wasn't in class, wasn't in the band. People said he had gone to a ranch out west to build up his strength. Which made some sense because he was so pale. He was just a boy in the band then, not yet my sweetheart, but I missed him. And was glad when he came back to school, after a couple of months, with some sun on his face.

I found out all about it years later, after he stood up to his old bully of a rich daddy and married me, after he started filling up our apartment with butterflies. At first it seemed innocent enough. He knew all about nature, could whistle bird songs, could say what kind they were when nobody else could see them flitting about in the trees. He'd capture butterflies, pin them to stiff cardboard, put them in box frames with cotton. At first, it was just on Saturdays; he'd be out there tramping around in the woods with his binoculars and butterfly nets. Then it was early in the morning weekdays before work. I had my job as a secretary for Dr. Newman and didn't pay much attention until butterflies started to take over the apartment. Our place was pretty small then, living room, kitchen, bedroom. And he just filled it up with butterflies, live ones wriggling in nets, dead ones, wings all sorts of colors, plus caterpillars, dead and alive. Strange smells all over the house. He hung glass-framed butterflies on all the walls, filled the shelves with messy, broken cocoons. Pretty soon heaps of wings covered the coffee table, the top of the refrigerator, the kitchen cabinets.

And then Pierce stopped, like he had wound down. He just sat in the middle of all that mess, staring at nothing, hardly talking.

I didn't know what to do; I was afraid to tell his parents. Afraid they'd blame me. They found out anyway because he'd stopped going to the Mill, where his dad had gotten him a job. So late one afternoon, old man Pierce burst in, took one look at the mess, and the next thing I knew, he carried my beautiful boy husband off in an ambulance.

That's when I found out it had happened before. It was a nervous breakdown, at least that's what his dad called it. They took him to a hospital down in North Carolina and put wires on the sides of his head and shocked him into getting better. His parents told folks he was traveling for business.

I'd done a lot of growing up before I ever married Pierce, keeping house for my hard-drinking daddy, getting myself a scholarship to secretarial school. But this was the worst. Pierce was the only person I'd ever loved except my mother who died when I was six. I loved his blunt fingers, his narrow body, the smell of starch his plaid shirts gave off, his sweet breath. I worried I'd somehow made him worse by letting him fill up the house with all that nature. That was a sign, and I'd missed it.

While he was gone, his parents bought us this house and moved me in. His mother told me she couldn't stand the idea of Pierce coming back to that tiny apartment where he'd had his breakdown. But the new place felt large and empty without him. And I was so lonely. I visited him several times before they decided to shock him, but that was worse than the loneliness. He just sat in a chair in his hospital room and stared at the TV. It didn't matter what the program was. I couldn't get him to talk or even look at me. It was awful. I thought he didn't love me anymore.

It didn't last forever. He came home and was his old self. Playing his clarinet, collecting, bird nests this time, but in an organized way in his "Museum."

Then Clare was born. My girl. Named for my mother. And he's been more or less okay ever since. He's had his ups and downs, of course, and once, when Clare was little, he had to go back for a shock treatment. But he's on a new medicine now and it's going well. To Clare he's the perfect father. She has no idea. And I want it to stay that way.

Wayne's at the door. Polite as pie. He's a good-looking boy. Six feet at least, floppy brown hair. Dark sleepy eyes. I see why Clare likes him.

"Where you off to, baby?" Pierce asks.

"A party," she says.

"Where?"

"Hunting Club."

"No," I say. The Hunting Club is a lump of stucco, squatting on the edge of the river. The members are mostly rednecks who shoot squirrel and rabbit and fancy themselves big game hunters.

"Wayne's playing for somebody's engagement party," she says.

"I don't like it," I say. "There'll be drinking and carrying on."

"I'll come," Pierce says.

Clare grabs him round the neck. I stare at them.

"I'll be the chaperone. Don't worry, honey."

It's only after he's climbed into the back seat of Wayne's Plymouth that I catch a glimpse of his clarinet case on the seat next to him.

Pierce plays a beautiful clarinet. He studied in New York. All the classics, *Flight of the Bumblebee*, Mozart's *Clarinet Concerto*. That was before we married. He'd had his heart set on being a musician, but his old man put his foot down, said you can't earn a decent living tootling on a horn. Sent him to work in one of the Mill offices, where the old man was president. I never knew what Pierce did exactly, only that he didn't like it. When his dad died, he left us enough money for Pierce to stop going to the Mill. He mostly stayed home and played his music and worked on his collections.

I wash the dinner dishes and pick up the *Ladies Home Journal*. But I've got that Hunting Club on my mind. I keep seeing the clarinet case on the back seat of Wayne's car. Pierce never plays in public, just has a friend or two come over occasionally to jam, as he calls it. He's a snob, really, about his music. So I'm thinking, *If he's planning to play his clarinet tonight, I want to hear it.* After about a half hour, I pull on my coat and back the Oldsmobile out of the garage.

I've seen the Club from the outside all my life but never had reason to go in. I open the door to a barn-like room full of crêpe paper streamers with big red cardboard hearts stapled to them and lots of loud music. Men in shirt sleeves and loosened ties are bouncing around with women done up in taffeta party dresses, blues and greens mostly, with full skirts out of net and black suede high heels. I recognize some of the patients from Dr. Newman's office, where I work, but they're too busy dancing to say hello. Besides, I'm looking all around for Clare and Pierce.

Wayne's up on a stage, banging away at the piano, a Buddy Holly tune I recognize, and laughing and talking to the dancers. Then, in a flash, he turns his head toward somebody in the band and starts nodding. And that's when I see Pierce. Up on the stage with all those boys. His eyes are closed, his square-tipped fingers are flying over the keys, and his head is swaying, all in perfect time with the guitars and piano. His face so serious. And Wayne's laughing and nodding.

After a minute or two people stop dancing and stand around the band watching Pierce, clapping to the beat, and belting out, *"Going faster than a roller coaster."* And there's Clare, up in front of the crowd, snapping her fingers with the others, her mouth moving. Pierce keeps playing that tune like it's the most natural thing in the world. When did *he* ever hear about Buddy Holly? The guitar player is grinning at him, and the short, skinny boy on banjo stops strumming long enough to let Pierce play solo. I push through the crowd, singing along with the rest of them, bumping into people, stepping on suede-covered toes. Trying to join my daughter. Getting the feel of it.

The clapping gets louder and louder. I see Wayne turn back to the piano. He tries a few chords but can't connect with Pierce's solo, so he stops and waits. I look at Pierce. His eyes are still closed, but now, instead of swaying to the rhythm, his whole body's jerking around. Buddy Holly is long gone. I have to reach Clare. Her eyes are fixed on her father, her cheeks are bright red, and she's stamping her feet with the beat. But the beat keeps changing and the tune seems to be lost. The noise in the room is getting louder. Pierce keeps on playing, faster and faster.

I don't know what to do.

It's Wayne who saves him. He picks up the microphone, walks over to Pierce and thanks him in a voice that drowns out the music. Pierce stops playing and looks around, like he's surprised.

Wayne says, "Well, folks, we've had a real treat here. Let's give a hand to the best woodwind player in the state of Virginia, Mr. Pierce Luther, Jr." He puts his arm around my husband's thin shoulders; Pierce gives a sideways grin and the two of them take a low bow.

"Thank you, Sir," Wayne says and walks him over toward me and Clare.

"What d'you think?" Pierce is beaming.

"Time to go," I say.

"No!" Clare says.

"Your Mom's right." Wayne puts his arms around Clare and Pierce, one on each side, and walks them to the door, with me following close behind.

"Thank you," I mutter, but he's gone, winding his way through the crowd, back to his piano.

On the way home Clare bounces around in the front seat next to me, talking a mile a minute.

"What about Dad's solo?"

"It was great. Most of it," I say. At least that's honest.

"Maybe my improvising was a bit sophisticated for the boys, huh?" Pierce chimes in from the back seat.

"Sounded like you were improvising on Mozart," I say.

"That wasn't Mozart. That was jazz."

"He was riffing on Buddy Holly," Clare says. "You're too tone deaf to hear it."

I let it go. Maybe this isn't what I think it is.

"Quick! What's the bird?"

It's early on Saturday morning, a week after the Hunting Club dance, and Pierce is peering through binoculars out the kitchen window, chirping: *Here I am-- in the tree-- look up-- at the top.*

"Red-eyed Vireo." Clare's answer is quick, automatic. She butters her toast, half asleep.

"Bingo!" Pierce has drilled those bird songs into her from the time she learned to talk. "Get dressed. Today's the day."

She's wide-awake now, binoculars in one hand, toast in the other, heading for the door. She's spent her childhood tramping the woods around Spotswood with her daddy, listening for bird songs, inspecting the forest floor for the telltale white splashes that might mean a nest, scrambling up oaks and elms and maples, easing the empty nests out of the tree limbs and carrying them home in a wicker basket lined with velvet. Whenever there are eggs, they wait until they're sure the nest is empty before making the snatch. I know all this because I went collecting with him before she was born. And I still occasionally go along, just to watch the two of them conspiring together, standing silent in the woods, waiting. I wait with them. Holding my breath.

This Saturday, I watch him closely. Ever since the party at the Hunting Club, I've felt kind of uneasy. So I call out, "Me too. I'm coming too."

Pierce heads the Dodge pickup south on Route 29. About thirty miles out of Spotswood, he swerves suddenly onto a dirt road. We bump along for several miles, red dust flying up in all directions, coating the windows.

"Where're you going?"

He laughs, a giddy sort of laugh.

And then he hits the brakes, jumps out of the car, and starts running.

"It's up there," he says, training his binoculars toward the top of a hill alongside the road. "Let's go."

He's running, up the base of the hill, kicking up red dust and brown pine needles.

By the time I get out of the car, he's a third of the way up the hill, hanging on to roots, a cotton mesh bag slung over his shoulder.

I look at the top of the hill through my binoculars. And there it is, on a low branch of a tree. A huge nest made of different size sticks with leaves spilling out the top. An owl's nest.

Pierce is inching up the hillside, grabbing roots, resting one foot at a time on rocks half-buried in the red dirt.

I call out in as calm a voice as I can manage, "Be careful, Pierce."

And then he's on the top of the hill, arms waving in triumph.

I look over at Clare. Her cheeks are bright. And she's grinning at her daddy. We watch Pierce stretch his hand up to the nest and carefully place it in the mesh bag. Then he starts scrambling down the hill.

In a flash, a Great Horned Owl swoops out of the air, claws outstretched. Clare and I race to the car. The mother lands on the branch of the tree where her nest was, screeching and screeching.

"Turn the motor on," Pierce yells as he half runs, half slides down to the bottom of the hill, binoculars swinging wildly around his neck, the bag held out beside him. He jumps into the front seat of the car, slamming the door just as the owl dive-bombs, crashing into the window beside him. For a split second, the bird glares in at us with large yellow eyes, then drops out of sight.

"Drive!" Pierce yells.

"Is she hurt?" Clare's voice is high pitched.

"Of course not," he says. "That bird is flying through the pine trees right now, swooping down on mice." He makes a perfect imitation of an owl's haunting call.

I want to scream at him, "It's not true. You know it's not true." But there's Clare.

"You think so?" she asks. She wants to believe.

Back home, Pierce sweeps two robins' nests aside to make space on the mahogany table for his latest prize.

"Look at the inside." Clare's voice is hushed.

I look down at downy feathers. The mother owl must have plucked them from her own breast. And there's squirrel fur in here. And then I see them. Two white perfectly formed eggs are resting on a cross hatch of downy feathers.

"What have you done?" I whisper.

Clare stares at her father. "We're not supposed to take 'em if there're eggs." She sounds close to tears.

"I'm sorry, baby," Pierce says. "I thought it was empty."

I don't believe him. I quickly put my arm around my daughter. "Even the experts make mistakes, honey," I say. "I'm sure your dad thought the nest was old."

Pierce smiles and nods.

Now that nesting season is in full swing, Clare is up early on Saturdays, out all day with her father, armed with binoculars, telescope, Sibley's, sandwiches. They come home after dark, exhausted, her cheeks flushed. She talks all through dinner, hardly eating anything. They're watching nests and the hatching of babies, red-tailed hawks, robins, cardinals. It's June; the woods are full of song.

I watch Pierce, but he seems calm, happy. Clare wants to be with him, that's all he needs. I tell myself, relax.

The owl's nest sits there in the middle of the mahogany table, large, messy, the eggs stone cold.

"Mama!" It's Clare's voice. Coming from Pierce's collections room.

I rush down the hall. The door is open. Mud and twigs, leaves and bark, thick on the floor, stop me.

Pierce is standing near the door. He looks at me, mouth open, eyes searching mine. I realize I've been expecting this. For weeks now. I've got to get her out of here before . . .

Then I see her. Her shoes are muddy and her sweater's torn. She's smiling, and for just one minute, I hope everything's going to be all right.

But there's something in her hands, something she's holding tight against her chest.

"It's my surprise," she says. Her eyes are bright, her voice high-pitched, excited. "It's because of the raccoons. Don't you see? I had to. The raccoons."

"Clare," I speak softly. "Sweetheart?"

"It's okay, Mama," she says, kicking at the pile of broken nests on the floor. "I just need a broom. It was too crowded in here. I had to make room. I just need a broom."

I reach for her.

She backs away. "Mama, where's the broom?"

Fear hangs heavy. Weighs me down. Stops my breath. "Sweetheart," I manage to whisper.

"I need to sweep." Her voice is frantic. "Look at all this mess."

But I'm not looking at the mess. I'm staring at the muddy fists she's stretching out to me. A broken handle of a purse-like nest dangles from her thumb.

She spreads open her fingers.

I don't want to look. I don't want to know. I want to hold her.

"Aren't they sweet, Mama? Aren't they perfect?"

Two pink featherless creatures lie limp in her hands, their tiny legs drawn up close to their bodies.

MASSIVE RESISTANCE

Massive Resistance was a policy adopted in 1956 by the Virginia State Government to block the desegregation of public schools mandated by the U.S. Supreme Court's 1954 decision in Brown v. Board of Education. Public schools were shut down in several cities throughout the state to prevent desegregation. Although the courts eventually overturned the policy, schools in Prince Edward County remained closed until the 1960s.

June 1957

Bryce Nolan breathed in the sweet scent of new grass as he headed through Harvard Yard. Buds exploded on the dogwoods. Scarlet blossoms crowned the crabapples. Like home. Almost. He glanced down at the brown bag in his dimpled fist. Another beer? Sure. He had time. He was feeling okay. Better than okay. In fact, he could almost forget the phone call last night.

"I just heard from Womack, son."

Oh shit. Just his luck his dad's campaign manager would land a job here as a Dean, snooping around, ratting on him.

"Yeah?"

"Says you're on probation."

"It's okay, dad. I'll take care of it."

"Says you're skipping class."

Was that all?

"I spent some time in the infirmary. Missed a few classes. Nothing I can't make up."

"I'm disappointed, son."

So Womack hadn't told him, which meant he didn't know. Bryce felt his plump shoulders relax. Those meetings *had* to be secret.

"You tell mama?"

"Not yet. You fix it, boy. You hear? We can't have your mama worrying about you."

"Yeah, I know." He wondered what she would say, his beautiful mama, if she knew the real reason he was cutting classes.

"You still swimming every day?"

"Yep." One more lie.

"Good. Gotta go. I'm counting on you. Don't let me down."

But he would. He didn't want to, but he would. It was just too hard to keep it up. Even though the good grades and prizes were the only way he knew to assuage his father's disappointment in the soft round bookworm that was his son. But now that he was over six hundred miles away, it no longer seemed important to knock himself out for his father's glory.

Back in his room he tossed the empty beer bottle in the trash and studied his doughy face in the mirror.

"She's a real sweetheart," his roommate Miles had told him. Which was code for not being pretty enough to get dates on her own. "You'll love her."

"Where's she from?"

"Some place in Virginia. Culpepper?"

He knew it. Apple country. A chubby farm girl from Virginia. He glanced down at the loose white flesh rolling over the waistband of his jockey shorts as he squirmed into a navy polo shirt. Who was he to judge? And it was just as well. The pretty ones always had excuses when he telephoned for a second date.

He tugged at the zipper of his madras Bermuda shorts, dug bare feet into his loafers, and reached for his keys.

One for the road?

Better not. He got grabby when he'd had too much. On the other hand, he felt on edge. A short bourbon wouldn't hurt him.

The wind hit him full in the face, warm, humid, as he raced his Buick convertible down route 16 toward Pine Manor Junior College. He loved that car. He'd had to work hard to persuade his dad he needed it to drive back and forth to Harvard, even though most students didn't have cars. On the radio, Elvis was growling, "I'm all shook up."

Why had he let the old man set him up as the town genius?

He was twelve when he got talked into entering the County Chess Tournament. Everybody else was older. High school slide-rule types, old guys who played in the park.

"Can't I wait 'til next year?" he'd begged his father.

"Are you kidding? Here's the thing, son. They're going to underestimate you. They'll be concentrating on each other, studying each other's plays from earlier tournaments. They won't pay attention to you, even the first time you make a smart move."

"If I get the chance."

"You will, boy. You're sharp. And by the time they've caught on to the fact that you're winning, they'll be too surprised to anticipate your moves."

"And what if I lose?"

"Don't let me hear that loser talk."

And when by some miracle he'd won, there was his father, Roger Nolan, Virginia State Senator, one arm holding him close, the other hand waiving the trophy over their heads, smiling for the photographer. The warmth, the lemony smell of his father's aftershave almost made his pre-tournament nausea worth it.

But later that night at the dinner table, as Bryce sat between his sister Liz, smiling up at him, half-shy and adoring, and his mother, who had filled his plate with barbequed chicken and mashed potatoes, his favorites, Roger Nolan said, "You need to work on your Sicilian defense. The State isn't going to be as easy as this one." He looked at his mother, waiting for her to say something like, *This is Bryce's night, let's celebrate.* But she just smiled.

And when he lost at the State level, because how could a thirteen-year-old win such a thing, his father was nowhere around.

What was pathetic was he'd tried. He'd tried so hard.

Liz hadn't been saddled with a superlative. Lucky Liz, he called her. His sweet, sweet sister.

"Fuck champions," he suddenly yelled over the radio, into the wind. The noon sun streamed in the front windshield, half blinding him; sweat dripped into his eyes. He hit the curve at 65 miles an hour. Too fast, he thought, slow down.

"Fuck the bookworm," he screamed. "Fuck the walking dictionary."

But his high-pitched laugh was drowned out by metal smashing, glass shattering, brakes screeching, a horn bleating.

June 1958

Betsy Nolan sat absolutely still in the spindle-backed rocking chair, except to lift her hand to turn the pages of *Middlemarch*, which lay open on her lap. Her dark hair, streaked with gray, was pulled back from her wide forehead into a bun; her cheeks were thin, silky; her large eyes, blue-gray.

If she concentrated on Dorothea and Mr. Casaubon, she could forget for hours at a time. Forget the telephone ringing that June afternoon a year ago. Ringing and ringing. The sheriff's polite voice on the line, asking for the Senator.

"He's not here. I'm his wife. Can you tell me what this is about?" The fear rising.

"I'm sorry, ma'am, but I must talk to the Senator. Would you please tell me where I can reach him?"

She had given him the office number, the private line, the number in Richmond, every number she could think of. And still the phone kept ringing and the sheriff kept asking for the Senator. So that when Roger finally came home, explaining that he'd unplugged his phone to write a speech, when he yelled, "No!" into the receiver, when he stared at her, still holding the phone, howling sounds beyond any meaning, she knew.

A year later and she still dreamed about him, Bryce, in the car, swerving, *not* crashing into the tree, running to her, laughing. Feeling herself light, buoyant for the split second before pulling the pillow over her face to stifle the screams.

Fortunately, there were whole days, weeks she couldn't remember. The sleeping pills, the dark rooms. Time lost.

And then the pathetic effort to resume her role as Roger's wife.

"Sweetheart, I need you," he'd said three months after the funeral. "The new governor is coming through to meet some of the school people. There's a small party."

"I don't have anything to wear." Where did that come from?

"Call Lucile. Have her sew you something new. Treat yourself." Practical Roger.

So she'd numbly picked through patterns and ordered several yards of lavender lace to cover a full taffeta skirt and black silk for the top.

The stout Lucile paused to remove several pins she held pinched between her lips. "You're a dream to sew for," she said. "Waist like a girl, and that dark hair goes so good with this black silk."

She huffed and puffed in Betsy's face, shoving pins into the delicate fabric with swollen pink fingers. "Miz Nolan, ain't you proud of the Senator, standing up for us like he is?"

Betsy nodded. She wasn't sure what Lucile was referring to and didn't want the burden of finding out.

"Yes ma'am, he's standing firm. And you're the lady for him."

She made her first public appearance six months after the funeral at the dedication of the new high school gymnasium, a graceless brick square of a building, plopped down on a raw field of red earth. She stood next to Roger, shivering in the damp December air, arranging her face to smile up at him while he gave his speech, which she almost completely ignored.

Almost. But then she heard him say, " . . . Now you and I know that certain people in this town want to use this handsome facility to bring about a mixing of the races." She was suddenly attentive. "But I give you my solemn promise . . ." She looked out over the starchy white faces bobbing up and down, nodding, frowning, and thought, *Who is this man?*

Back home she confronted him. "That sounded like segregationist talk."

He didn't meet her eyes. "Well, I've been wanting to tell you, sweetheart, but you've been so, I don't know, distant. It's something of a feather in my cap."

"What is?"

"It's the Governor's baby, you know that. Massive Resistance. That's how he got elected."

"How's that a feather in *your* cap?" But she knew.

"Well, he's asked me to play a leadership role here in Southside."

Her charismatic Roger? The idealistic Harvard student who had pulled her into his orbit and taken total possession of her years ago when she was a Vassar girl? Wooed her with his dark eyes and high cheek bones and cleft chin, his smooth spare body, his lilting southern accent. The way we treat the people down south is just wrong, he'd said, and something had to be done about it.

"*You're* fighting integration? You?"

"Not really." His eyes shifted away from hers. "Look honey, I'm representing my part of the state, the folks who elected me."

"I thought you were supposed to lead them."

"Give me time. I can turn it around. You'll see."

He was smiling, watching her now with careful eyes.

"What happened to the man who brought me here after college to 'knock some heads together,' as you put it, and usher in the future?"

Roger flinched. "Give me a break, Betsy. You know as well as I that you have to get elected in order to make a change."

"And you plan to make a change, as you say, by buying into racist ideas like this Massive Resistance?" she said.

"I can't do anything if I can't get elected," he shot back.

She realized she was too tired to take him on. At just that moment she no longer cared.

And so she had quietly, permanently slipped away from the only life that was real to her husband. She avoided political dinners, stopped going to Bridge Club, which she'd always secretly hated, stayed home from the Baptist Church. Florine, the maid, told the visitors, prying do-gooders as well as the genuinely sympathetic, that she wasn't home or was ill. Roger cautioned his curious constituents to be patient, that she was taking the death hard. The retreat to the bland impersonal guest room, to George Eliot and Jane Austen and Henry James, had been gradual. At home, Florine cooked the meals, did the shopping, cleaned the house, without instruction, without asking questions. Liz had her life at the high school. So that once Betsy renounced her role as political wife, there was a vast silence. Initially, she had tried to fill it with projects, a crocheted pillow, a vegetable garden that first terrible summer. The final project, sorting through a large cardboard box of family photos, almost destroyed her.

A faded photo of Bryce, staring, unsmiling, at a birthday cake with six lit candles, his soft cheeks already too round.

"Make a wish," someone shouts. "Quick. Before they go out." It's Roger, outside the photo, his voice ungentle. There are other faces outside the photo, small boys mostly, dressed in white shirts and brown corduroy knickers, their faces red, their hair standing up in wet clumps from racing up and down the curved staircase, throwing peanuts and popcorn at each other. At him.

"Hurry. Blow them out."

But he doesn't. He looks at her. I told you, his eyes say. His eyes already brimming with tears. Then he runs. Out of the room, up the stairs.

"Too much party," Roger says into the silence. "Who wants to blow out the candles?"

But she doesn't wait to see. She's on the stairs, in the hall, opening the door to an empty room.

"Come out, Bryce," she calls gently. She's been here before. She reaches under the double decker bed and runs her fingers over a soft arm.

"I'm sorry," she says. "You were right. We won't do it again."

"Daddy will make me."

And then she's sitting in the spindle-back rocking chair holding him, wiping his tears with the edge of the cowboy and Indian bedspread she has pulled off the bed and wrapped him in, humming.

"I hate them."

"They're not bad boys," she says. "They're just not your friends."

She holds him tight against her.

And she could have held Roger at bay, could have listened for words her awkward son didn't say. The details of her failure kept her staring into dark space, robbed of sleep, night after night. Signing him up for tennis lessons, when she knew he hated them, backing up his father when he begged her not to have to compete in chess tournaments, nagging him about too many desserts. Finally, at six o'clock one morning, the back of her eyes aching from lack of sleep, she threw the photos back into the carton, boxed up Bryce's trophies and books and shoved them all into the closet in Bryce's bedroom. She hadn't opened the bedroom door again.

She began to take naps in the upstairs guest room, then to have Florine bring her meals up there. Now she slept alone in the four-poster mahogany bed that had belonged to Roger's Alabama grandmother. Once a week, she left the house to walk the three short blocks to the public library. Then back to the dark, silent house, bearable only because she had sealed off her son's memories.

February 1959

That afternoon, like every afternoon after school, Liz lit up the house. First, the bronze chandelier in the hall, next the four Chinese table lamps in the living room, then the crystal chandelier over the dining room table. She drew back the maroon and gray flowered drapes to let in what sun remained in the late winter sky. She didn't have to light up the kitchen. Fluorescent tubes shone harshly on the straight-backed woman with cocoa-colored skin who was standing over the sink.

"How you, baby?" Florine looked up from the potatoes she was peeling.

"I'm okay. What's for dinner?" Liz asked.

"Pork chops, scalloped potatoes, snap beans from the freezer. You hungry?"

"Maybe later. You need anything?"

"I'm short on flour and milk."

"Okay. I'll run down the street in a minute."

"Get yourself some of that butter pecan ice cream while you're there."

"You mean, get *you* some."

Florine laughed. "How you make out on that French test, baby?"

"Lousy. Don't tell Daddy."

"What do'y think I am?"

"Mama resting?"

It wasn't really a question and Florine didn't bother to answer.

Liz opened the door of her mother's room cautiously, as if she half expected something embarrassing to spring out of a corner. But it was the same colorless, featureless room it had always been. Beige carpet, beige curtains fully drawn, the off-white Martha Washington bedspread on Grandmother Bryce's bed, the wrought iron reading lamp, and the rocking chair where her mother now sat.

"Hi Mama."

Betsy Nolan looked up from the book in her lap, rubbed the bridge of her nose above her glasses, and stretched her pale lips into a smile. Liz was struck, as she often was, by her mother's beauty. No make-up. No need for it. It was a beauty neither she nor her brother had inherited. Unlike her tall willowy mother, Liz was short, her legs slightly bowed, her brown hair coarse, straight. Only her smile, her father's smile, and his dark eyes, saved her from being outright homely.

"How was school?" Betsy asked.

Liz sat on the bed, as she always did, and tried to interest her mother in the latest craze of gold circle pins the girls were wearing.

"Where's your list, Mama?" she finally asked, when it was clear her mother was only pretending to listen.

Betsy pulled an index card from the copy of *David Copperfield* in her lap and handed it to Liz.

"Are you going today?"

"Sure. I've got some groceries to pick up for Florine, and I can stop by the library on the way. Any returns?"

Betsy pointed to a stack of thick books with worn covers on the bedside table.

"Thank you, dear." She settled her glasses on the narrow bridge of her thin, straight nose and returned to her book.

Some days Liz could barely remember there had been another life, a different mother. She almost forgot the long hot summer days at Nags Head, white caps crashing over her, salt water in her nose and mouth, laughing, laughing with her big brother, his bathing trunks slipping below his bulging belly.

To stave off the pain, she averted her eyes from the large, framed photograph in the entrance hall of the high school where she was now a junior. "In Memory Of Bryce Templeton Nolan." The tassel from his graduation cap half-covering his pasty, solemn face, an uneasy valedictorian. At home she rushed, unseeing, past his bedroom door, a door opened only by Florine, and only once a month, to dust and vacuum.

But sometimes she'd see lumbering toward her, in the crowded halls of her high school, a hulking shape of a boy with a canvas book bag slung over his shoulder, and she'd feel as if she were suffocating.

She'd been in her ninth grade history class when it happened, watching a movie about Bethlehem Steel, one of those tedious educational films where the voice was all wobbly and the picture jumped on the makeshift screen. She was taking the opportunity of the dark room and her inattentive teacher to write a note to Toby Watkins when she looked up and found herself staring into Mr. Harrison's shiny red face. The Principal. He was talking, but the roar of the projector and the narrator's gravelly voice were so loud she couldn't hear him.

And then, "I need to take you home."

"What is it?" she kept asking as he walked her out of the dark classroom into the blinding sunlight. "What's wrong?" Begging, pleading all the way home in his Jeep station wagon.

"Don't worry. Your dad wants to see you. I'm sure it's nothing" was all he would say. She'd hated him ever since.

Then she was running into the living room. To her father, who was holding out his arms. His face all distorted, not his face at all.

She screamed, "No," and pushed against him, twisted in his grip.

March 1959

When the crushing pain began to ease, Roger Nolan experienced a lightness of being that surprised him. His slightly hunched shoulders relaxed, his smile was no longer forced, his heels, when he walked from fundraiser to ceremony to party meeting, bounced off the pavement. He had loved his son. And not just for his brilliance, although that's what Betsy believed. She was wrong. He'd loved the way the boy needed him when he was small, the way he looked to Roger for approval. The way he'd lift up his arms to be held when he was frightened. Those memories tortured Roger. But he was too honest a man not to admit that his love for Bryce had been mixed with disappointment, sometimes even fury. At his son's unhappy fat face, his unsociable nature. Most recently at his poor performance at his own Alma Mater.

And then there was his irritating purity. This was Virginia, for Christ's sake, southern Virginia, and he, Roger Nolan, was its representative. Everyone he knew, everyone who could vote for him wanted segregation. But history was *not* on the side of his complacent constituents; he had figured that out years ago. And he planned to pick up the pieces and lead the way when the courts and, more important, business interests forced the south to give up its losing battle. In the meantime, he represented southern Virginia, for better, for worse. They weren't bad people. But they hadn't gone to integrated schools, and they were damned if their children were going to.

"Folks prefer to be with their own kind," was how they put it. "Ask my girl; she'll tell you."

And it wasn't as if they didn't have schools of their own.

"Their schools aren't as good," Bryce had reminded him. Sixteen-year-old Bryce, at the breakfast table. Two years ago.

"Hold on there, boy," he'd said. "What do you know about it?"

"You got me that job last summer, mending the books at the schools. I know what I saw."

"What was that?" But he knew. He'd seen it himself.

"The books at Luther Burbank were the books we white kids threw away. The pages were torn, the spines all broken, a mess."

He'd sat there, watching his boy stuff his fat cheeks with bacon and eggs and cereal and muffins.

"God-dammit, Bryce! Don't eat so fast."

Those were the memories that cut deep. The shamed look on the boy's face, the eyes avoiding his. He should have agreed with his son. Luther Burbank *was* dilapidated, the books out of date, the teachers overwhelmed. But he didn't. He couldn't. He was too caught up in the political reality of the people who put him in office.

The problem was, the NAACP was organizing to integrate the schools, and the white folks in Spotswood were talking about setting up a segregated private academy for their kids. He didn't agree with them, but these were the folks who voted for him. He had to take their side. He didn't have a choice.

He wished Betsy could see it like he did. He wanted those intelligent blue-gray eyes smiling up at him as he worked the crowds. God, he loved her. It drove him crazy seeing her sitting in that room, practically in the dark, day after day.

He'd loved her right from the beginning. It was 1935, the year he graduated from high school.

She was sitting, all alone, on the expansive wooden porch of the Old Colony Inn at Nags Head. Rocking back and forth in one of the dozens of white rockers set out for guests and gazing out toward the ocean with eyes the same color as the Atlantic. Her dark hair was coiled on top of her head in thick braids, leaving her long, satin neck exposed. He even remembered what she was wearing: a high-necked white blouse and a soft dark cotton skirt. But what had stopped him, what had made him sit down in the rocking chair next to her, was the ivory white of her skin. The searing North Carolina sun hadn't touched it.

"I'm Roger Nolan," he'd said and then just stared at her, stunned by all that ivory skin into silence.

The girl's quick smile suggested she was eager to meet someone, anyone, who might provide distraction from the boredom she didn't bother to conceal.

"I'm Betsy Templeton, visiting with my aunt Evelyn. She's sweet but awfully old, and she didn't know what to do with me in Greensboro. That's where she lives. So she packed us up and took off for the seashore. And here I am."

"Is it so bad?" he asked.

"You'll think I'm horrid."

"Try me."

"Well, to tell you the truth, yes. It's my first visit to the southern states, and I don't know what I was expecting, but I find it all mystifying. And, I have to say, backward."

Roger laughed. "You're right about backward. But don't you think the sand here is just about the finest you ever put your foot on?"

She admitted the sand was soft and white and she liked to float in the warm waves. But she was a New England girl and she was bored.

"Oh yeah? What do you do up in New England to keep from getting bored?"

"I don't know. Play tennis, sail, all kinds of things." She watched him rocking back and forth before she spoke, in a tone almost challenging. "And I'm going to college in a month."

"Goodness me. Where?" The girls he knew went to finishing schools; hardly any went to a real college.

"You probably never heard of it. It's called Vassar."

He laughed out loud. "Vassar? No kidding." He jumped up and faced her, forcing her to stop rocking. "Then, I bet you've heard of Harvard."

She smiled up at him with large gray-blue eyes. "Well, pleased to meet you, Harvard," she said.

They quickly established that they were fervent New Dealers even though, or maybe because, their parents disapproved. Roger confessed his dream of one day running for the U.S. Congress; Betsy wanted, in some ill-defined way, to help the poor. But it wasn't dreams of the future that changed his life that summer. It was the taste of salt on her lips, the sting of the hot North Carolina sun, the powdery sand on the cool dunes at night. It was slogging clumsily to the top of the dunes, then racing, tumbling to the flat beach below, Betsy holding onto her wide brimmed straw hat with one hand, the other clinging to Roger's sunburned arm. There were millions of places to hide in the dark sand, behind the dunes, in crevices on top. They couldn't stop talking; they couldn't stop touching. At the beginning, the aunt from Greensboro felt obligated to accompany her niece whenever she left the hotel for the beach, and when Roger came to call, she chose a rocking chair on the porch near, but not too near, the infatuated couple. Ultimately, however, she relaxed her vigilance, impressed by the supposed safety net of Harvard. Roger's high school friends, who had driven down from Spotswood with him, marveled at his good luck. But Roger knew it was for the rest of his life.

Once in college, they filled in the blanks, his ambition, her devotion to him, his plan to go back south and make a better world, her trust that he could do it.

In the years that followed, Roger never stopped marveling at her beauty, her cool charm, her helpless love for their clumsy boy. He loved her, and her distance after Bryce's death pained him, more, if he let himself admit it, than the boy's death.

Finally, out of desperation, he got her an appointment with Ashby Fuller, even though he thought psychiatry was baloney. And she'd gone dutifully.

"How'd it go?" he'd asked afterwards.

"Fine, I guess."

"What'd he say?"

"Not much."

"Did he give you any pills or anything?"

"No."

"When are you going again?"

"I'm not." And that was it. Roger tried to get Ashby to tell him what was wrong with his wife, but the man had refused. Patient confidentiality.

She'll come round, he thought, eventually. Meanwhile, Roger Nolan considered himself a practical man. He didn't like this Massive Resistance movement. Thought it was wrong-headed, doomed. But, like it or not, it was his only way forward. And Roger Nolan was going forward.

April 1960

Liz Nolan raced her red Schwinn down the hills and around the sharp curves of her tree-lined neighborhood. The maples were in first tender-green leaf. She couldn't get enough of the sun, the sweet air, the soft breeze in her face. The relief after the dark house, her sad mama. A stack of books was in her basket on the handlebars.

She loved the old nineteenth century house on Main Street which served as Spotswood's library, loved the smell of the books, the hush in the spacious cedar paneled, book-lined room, the polished cherry-wood tables over to the left where several women sat reading, the balcony up above with its painted white bannister and bookshelves to the ceiling. They called the old building the Memorial Mansion because Robert E. Lee was supposed to have slept there at some point during the War. Mrs. Wyatt, who had presided over the library for as long as Liz could remember, had read all those books. At least that's what Liz had concluded because she never ran out of suggestions or enthusiasm.

"I don't think your mama has read Trollope lately," Mrs. Wyatt said as Liz handed her the returns.

The diminutive, bone-thin librarian spent the next ten minutes pulling books off the shelves and whispering to Liz the delicious intricacies of each plot. Despite her fragile appearance, she moved briskly about the old building, hopping up and down ladders, stacks of books in her wiry arms.

Liz was looking forward to spending a half hour or so, sprawled on the grass in front of the library, sampling the books, then choosing one and losing herself in her mother's world of nineteenth century English manners. So after checking out as many books as she could handle on her bicycle, she headed for the door.

But the massive oak door was blocked. Four boys stood, shoulder to shoulder, in front of it. Boys about her age, seventeen or eighteen years old, dressed in ill-fitting sports jackets and dark blue ties. They barely noticed her because they were looking all around the library, as if they'd never seen so many books, as if they didn't know what to do next.

And they were boys from Luther Burbank.

"May I help you?" Mrs. Wyatt slipped in front of Liz, pushing her back with a hand that was surprisingly strong.

"We'd like some books, ma'am." The tallest one stared down at the librarian and thrust his hands out to his sides, palms facing backwards, as if to silence the others. Later, when her father asked her to describe this boy, Liz couldn't remember what color his coat was. All she remembered was his dark skin and big hands.

"I'm afraid I can't help you with that," Mrs. Wyatt said. Her voice was soft. "You must know this is a whites only library."

"It's a public library, ma'am," the boy said. "And we're the public." The other boys were beginning to mumble and shift from foot to foot, but their spokesman kept them in check with his long, outspread fingers.

"There's a branch of this library on Calhoun Street." Mrs. Wyatt's voice squeaked midway through the sentence. "You can get books there."

"There ain't any good books there, lady," one of the other boys said, stepping out in front of the spokesman and staring down into Mrs. Wyatt's face, which was white as powder. "It's a mess."

"I'm very sorry. But I can't let you in this library."

"We're from Burbank," the tall one said. "We need books for school."

"If you tell me what books you want, I can send them to Burbank," she said.

But it was too late. They were moving forward, shoulder to shoulder, forcing the librarian backwards into the room. Liz jumped out of the way.

The handful of women who had been reading stood up and without a word formed a frightened huddle behind one of the library tables. Liz was sure something terrible was about to happen. But she just stood there, in a trance, and watched these boys march over to a shelf on the wall opposite the ladies. Without a word, they began to pull out books at random, glance at a few pages, then stack the books carefully on a nearby table.

Within minutes sirens were screaming and six policemen pounded through the door.

"Everybody stay where you are," one of them yelled.

The boys continued to pull books from the shelf, but Liz could tell from the way they looked at each other that they were frightened.

"I said stay where you are!" the policeman yelled. "And put your hands up."

One by one, skinny brown arms waved in the air.

"We have the right to be here," the tall one said. But his shrill voice lacked confidence.

"You're trespassing, you scum," the officer bellowed. "Cuff 'em," he ordered his men.

Minutes later, the men pushed the boys out the door, their wrists handcuffed behind their backs, their heads down. One of them was crying.

A woman who had witnessed the whole thing patted the librarian on the back. "Good for you," she said. "I was frightened half out of my wits."

The other women clustered around Mrs. Wyatt, nodding, clutching at her trembling hands. She didn't say a word, just sat down at the cherry wood table and put her head in her hands. Liz wanted to say something to comfort her but didn't know how.

Afterwards, riding her bicycle back through the leafy streets of Spotswood, Liz couldn't get those boys out of her mind. They looked so scared, and they were so orderly, pulling the books from the shelves, stacking them neatly. She would have expected them to talk back or start to run once the police showed up. But they stayed polite the whole time. She knew what her father would say. Those boys had no place in the white library, and maybe they shouldn't have been there. But putting them in handcuffs? Taking them off in a police car? Suppose it had been Jess. She began to pedal faster. She needed to talk to Florine.

Florine, ready for work in her gray cotton uniform with the starched white collar and apron, stared at a tall, scrawny boy with close-cropped frizzled hair.

"You know anything bout them boys getting the white libary closed?"

Jess looked up from his cornflakes. "I heard of it."

"Well, you stay out of it, you hear me?"

"What you mad at me for? I ain't involved." The boy got up from the metal-topped table, which was shoved up against the wall, and looked square into his mother's eyes. His mattress, a blanket tucked neatly under the sides, was on the opposite side of the room, and in between bed and table was a wooden bench and two armchairs, upholstered in faded wool plaid. The wood floor of the small, crowded room was bare.

"You better not be. This the best job I ever had, and you ain't going to mess with it."

Jess laughed. "The old honky!"

"That old honky's gonna pay for your college long as you behave yourself."

"I behave."

"Well, don't let me catch you making trouble for the Senator."

"Mama, listen to you talk. You know them boys are right."

"I don't know nothing," she said. "I keep my opinions to myself, and I'll thank you to do the same."

After Jess left for school, Florine sat on the wooden bench for a few minutes, staring out the window at a black and white mutt running down the unpaved road in front of her house, barking.

She thought about the mothers. What they go'n do, knowing their boys are in jail and they can't do nothing about it. Mr. Nolan *could* do something about it; but he won't. He treated her decent, but he had no notion how folks lived. And with all the sadness in that house after that business with Mr. Bryce, he'd never know. Those boys were foolish going into that libary. But brave too.

"Lord, keep my boy safe," she prayed under her breath, as she pulled herself up from the bench and headed down the dirt road to the bus stop. "Just keep him safe."

"It's a damn shame," Roger announced, barging into his wife's room. "Some kids from Luther Burbank forced their way into the Memorial

Mansion after school and started taking books. John Watson had to close the place down."

Betsy jumped up. "What do you mean, close it down?"

"Just what I said, honey. Mrs. Wyatt asked them to leave, they refused, and she called the police."

"Liz told me that part, but I didn't know that stuffed shirt mayor had closed the library." She turned to face the window; she needed fresh air

"It might be good for you," Roger said, opening the window. "Get you out of this room."

You have no idea, she thought.

"What are you going to do?" she asked, her back to him, breathing in the outdoors.

"Right now, we're letting things simmer down. You remember this happened before when that school teacher from Luther Burbank tried to check out a book. It was a mess; all those rednecks storming the place. If we open the library now, they will be back and there'll be violence. So we'll wait for the lawsuit and work something out."

"The law takes a long time."

"Time is on our side, honey."

"I can't," she said.

"What's that mean?"

She didn't bother to explain.

She rarely left her room after that. She still had books, in the house and on regular order from Book of the Month Club, but she didn't read the paper or listen to the radio. She didn't ask Roger about the library. She didn't want to hear it.

June 1960

Then one summer afternoon two months after the mayor closed the library, Florine announced, "Miz Nolan, there's a man at the door."

"What man?"

"I guess it's a boy. Says he wants to see you."

"You know what to tell him." Why was the woman bothering her with this?

"Yes'm. I did already."

"Well then, would you please close my door?"

Florine just stood there. "Miz Nolan, he says he was a friend of Mr. Bryce."

Betsy let out a sharp cry. "Tell him to see Mr. Nolan in his office downtown," she said.

"I already done that, ma'am. He wants to see you."

She searched her maid's impassive face. "No!"

"I told him to leave, told him you won't see him. But he won't go way."

Betsy started to close the door, but then she thought, suppose he's telling the truth. Suppose he was . . . She had to see. Her legs trembled as she started down the stairs.

"Mrs. Nolan?"

A young man was standing in the front hall, at the bottom of the stairs, peering up at her from under heavy black eyebrows, not smiling. His shoulders under his rumpled seersucker jacket were slightly hunched, his skin pale, his scrawny arms hung limp.

"Please, Mrs. Nolan." His voice was high pitched and nasal. New York?

She called out sharply. "Florine!"

The boy backed away, swiping at his sweaty forehead with his sleeve. "I'm George Bradstreet, ma'am." The words rushed out. "Bryce's friend. I mean, *was* his friend."

She was frightened now. He could be anybody. Pretending to be her son's friend.

"What do you want?"

"I'm part of the protest, Mrs. Nolan."

Betsy walked down the stairs to the bottom and faced him. "I don't understand."

"The protest." His voice was insistent. "We were down at the library, holding up signs, trying to get it back open. But the cops showed up and started arresting all the protesters. I started to protest, and the cop told me I better get my ass, sorry ma'am, out of there or I'd go to jail too."

The cops? What was he talking about? She looked at her maid.

"I been hearing about it, ma'am," Florine said.

The boy began talking very fast. "A bunch of us from Harvard came down here this summer to join the fight for integration." He suddenly looked so young, so innocent.

"That has nothing to do with me," she said.

"Bryce was one of us. Only he didn't tell you because he was scared it would leak out and somebody would use it against his dad."

No.

He pulled from his pocket a single sheet of paper, folded so many times it was beginning to tear.

"This is our manifesto," he said.

Manifesto! What a child, she thought. What an absolute baby.

He handed it to her and pointed to a name at the bottom. Bryce Nolan. It was his handwriting, slanted to the left, letters close together.

She struggled to get her breath. "Where did you get this?"

"He said you might understand — what we're doing."

"I don't," she whispered. "I don't understand."

"He was my friend." The boy's voice was thick.

She wanted to run back up the stairs, pick up her book, get this boy out of her house. Instead, something made her ask, "What did you say your name is?"

"George. George Bradstreet."

It sounded vaguely familiar. Maybe when Bryce was home for Christmas? He could be. She didn't know.

"Maybe some time you could visit my husband in his office," she said.

"I'll do that, Mrs. Nolan. I'm sorry to bother you."

"Take him to the kitchen," she said to Florine. "Get him some ice tea."

She heard the boy whisper, "Thank you," to Florine.

"Thank you for what?" Betsy asked Florine, her voice sharp.

"I think he meant it for you, ma'am," Florine said.

Ten minutes later the door to the kitchen burst open. Roger Nolan filled the room, tall, imposing, fierce. His dark eyes fixed on the young man perched on the edge of a straight-backed wooden chair. George Bradstreet sprang up and stuck out his hand. Florine disappeared into the pantry.

"I got a call just now from my wife," Roger said, ignoring the offered hand. "Says you came to my house uninvited, claiming to be a friend of my son."

"I'm sorry if I offended her, sir. But it's true I was Bryce's friend, good friend. I'm George Bradstreet. From New York." They stood in the middle of the kitchen staring at each other.

"You in trouble with the police?"

"I hope not."

"You involved in that business downtown?"

George hesitated. "I was part of a march."

"A lot of folks got arrested."

"I know. That's when I left."

"And ran for safety here? To my house?" Roger's voice was sharp.

"I'm sorry, sir," George said. "I guess that wasn't too smart."

"Damned right, it wasn't smart. You put my wife, who isn't well, in a terrible position. Dangerous even."

"I'll leave right now." George headed for the kitchen door.

"Wait."

George turned back.

"You say you knew Bryce?"

"Yes sir."

Roger's dark eyes searched his face. "I'll check that out," he said. "Meanwhile, do not disturb my wife again. Do not come here again. Ever. Understood?"

"Yes sir." And he was gone.

Roger took the stairs two at a time. Betsy was standing at the window when he rushed into her room.

"I got rid of him," he said. He tried to put his arms around her. She held herself stiff, staring out the window.

"He could be telling the truth," she murmured.

"I'll find out. But even if he did know Bryce, he had no business coming here scaring you like that."

She turned to face him. "You're right. It scared me."

"He won't be back, honey. I promise."

He felt her body soften against him. He wanted to take hold of her, pull her into him.

She looked into his eyes. "How do *you* feel?"

"Right now I'm mostly angry that he came here and compromised you."

She smiled and pulled herself away from him. "You mean, compromised *you.*"

He ignored that. "It's you I worry about," he said.

She turned back to the window.

"I want it to be true," she said.

"I love you, Betsy," he said.

She didn't answer. And Roger knew he'd been dismissed.

"You seen Jess?" Florine was pushing through tangled knots of boys, not just brown ones, white ones too, blocking the street, shouting, "Unlock the doors," shouting "Books for freedom," chanting, chanting until she thought her head would burst.

Then suddenly sirens screaming full blast. Cop cars speeding into the crowd, thick-necked bullies in uniform jumping out, waving Billy sticks. A boy went down close to where Florine was standing, a kid, maybe twelve years old, his head bloody. She felt herself being shoved to the side of the road as screaming boys raced to escape the police. Jess. Where was he? They'd been doing it for two days now, the cops. Driving their cars right into the middle of the protest. Picking up the boys, children really, carting 'em off to jail. Beating up on the ones who fought back. Where was Jess?

Somebody had to stop it. Maybe the Senator, if he came down here with his megaphone. He'd been known to do it, get up on a stump and yell at a crowd to move back. Mr. Big Shot. But what if he spotted Jess? Or her?

Then suddenly there was Jess, standing on the outside of the crowd. Thank you, God. Staring, his mouth open.

"Get your black ass home," she shouted in his ear.

"What you doing here?"

"Getting you out of trouble."

He followed her, at a distance so it wouldn't look like he was a mama's boy, but he followed her.

Back home, safe, she could hear the sirens, the loud voice, not the Senator's, on the megaphone, the screaming.

"That could be *you* screaming," she said.

Jess lay down on his mattress and stared up at the ceiling. "I'm careful, Mama. The cops don't pay me no mind."

"You stay out there yelling and carrying on and see what mind they pay," she said.

"I gotta be involved," he said. "Dr. King, he says the time is now. And you know he's right."

She wanted to say, I know. I'm the one that sits in Reverend Martin's Bible class every Sunday and hears him talk protest, protest, protest. I know bout the marches. I want to be out there bad as you.

But she didn't say that. Instead she said, "Well, Dr. King's not your mama, I am, and I say you can't be out there getting beat up and going to jail."

But she knew he'd be back.

"Where you off to, honey?"

Liz stopped short. Florine was standing near the entrance hall of the unlit living room, in her broad-brimmed straw hat, ready to leave for home.

"I'm meeting some friends."

"At this hour?" It was close to eight o'clock.

"What is this, the third degree?"

Florine laughed. "Somebody got to look after you." Poor little girl. No mama to speak of.

"Well, maybe I just won't go," Liz said, slipping out of her red cotton sweater.

"I reckon you'll just wait till I'm gone?" Florine looked closely at the girl. Liz stood silent.

"Cause I'm betting you going to the protest downtown."

"What protest?"

"Don't you give me that 'what protest.' You know what I'm talking bout."

Liz sat down on the gray velveteen sofa, her sweater bunched up beside her, and looked up at Florine.

"You know you can't be out there," Florine said. But she was thinking, I wish I hadn't seen her. Let her go on out there, show up her daddy for a change.

"Why not?" Liz asked.

Pretending all innocence.

"Well, to start with, it's dangerous."

"I want to help."

"Well, it ain't going to help nobody if you get your daddy in trouble."

"If Bryce were here, he'd go."

"If Bryce were here, he'd tell *you* to stay home." God help me, she thought, I got to save this one too. She was dog tired. She wanted to shove the girl's sweater to the side and sit down on the sofa. But she couldn't.

"I want to do *something*."

"Well, you can't go prancing about in public. You'll have them reporters all over you." Course, she'd never thought of that, poor baby. "You remember Miss Foster?"

Liz looked up, surprised. "The old chemistry teacher, that Miss Foster?"

"That's the one."

"What about her?"

"You might look her up."

"What for?"

"I'm not saying another word."

"Look her up where, Florine?"

"I bet she's in the book."

"The phone book?" Liz thought a minute. "Are you saying Miss Foster's protesting?"

"I already said too much. Now go on upstairs."

Liz just sat there.

"Look here. If you go to that protest and I saw you leaving, I'll be in hot water."

"I won't tell."

"He'll ask, and you won't lie."

Liz stood up and put her arms around Florine's neck. "Okay. Next time I'll make sure you aren't around."

"Whatever. Now get on upstairs like a good girl."

July 1960

Two weeks after George Bradstreet visited the Nolans, he appeared at Roger's law office, once again in the rumpled seersucker jacket. But this time he was wearing a white, buttoned shirt and striped tie.

"Come on in," Roger said, leading the way past a grand mahogany roll-top desk. Roger eased himself into a leather armchair next to a table on which stacks of paper were piled.

"Sit down," he commanded.

George backed himself onto a plush blue sofa, his eyes never leaving the older man.

"Thank you for inviting me here," he said.

"I said I'd check up on you," Roger said.

George laughed nervously. "Yeah? Did I pass?"

"Looks like you're telling the truth. About knowing my son." Roger's voice trembled slightly. 1960 was Bryce's class. His boy would be finished with Harvard by now. Struggling to control his voice, Roger said, "I understand you just graduated."

"Yes sir." George smiled for the first time and looked around the room. A red Oriental carpet covered most of the dark hardwood floor. And drawings hung on the gray walls, drawings of buildings mostly. Colonial houses with columns, including one of Monticello. And one of those drawings of a tobacco barn that hangs on the wall of every white southerner's house.

"My wife tells me you boys are down here plotting to save the South from itself," Roger said.

"I don't know about that, sir, but Bryce was one of us."

"Well, the little son of a bitch," Roger muttered under his breath.

George hesitated, then spoke in a rush of words. "Our goal is to get the library back open."

"*Our* goal?"

"A few of us from college."

Roger's eyes narrowed. "You came to my house. I assume it wasn't just a friendly visit. What do you want from me? "

George looked directly into the black eyes. "Nothing, sir. I was scared that day when the cops showed up at the protest. First thing I thought of was Bryce. So I came to your house. It was a bad idea."

"It was a terrible idea."

"I know, but Bryce talked about his mother a lot. I thought she might . . ."

About *her.* Of course, Roger thought. I hate to think what he said about me.

"You can't visit her. You know that."

"I know."

"So? What *do* you have in mind?"

"I'm still marching."

"I figured. You know what they call you boys? 'Outside agitators.' Nothing gets the police more riled up than white boys coming down south and telling them their business."

George nodded. "They've made that clear. But I'll keep protesting until the library is integrated. It's what I came down here for."

Roger frowned. "What else are you doing?"

"Getting folks to sign petitions. Writing letters."

"What kind of letters?"

"Letters about the lousy selection of books in the black library."

Roger frowned. "What do you know about that?"

"I've seen it myself. And I've been going to meetings at Reverend Martin's house. He's signing the letters I'm writing. And some of the Burbank teachers are signing them."

"Where're you living?"

"There are white people who put me up."

"Really?"

They sat in silence for a few minutes.

Then Roger leaned forward once again fixing George with fierce, dark eyes. "Son, has it occurred to you that a town without a library can't attract new business?"

George grinned. "It has now."

Roger stood up. "You didn't hear it from me."

George jumped up and held out his hand for Roger to shake just as Roger reached out to lead him to the door. They bumped against each other and laughed awkwardly.

"Look, George," Roger said, "if it ever gets out that we've talked about this letter business, I'll deny knowing anything about it. I'll say you came here under false pretenses taking advantage of my grief. You understand?"

George nodded and picked up his jacket to leave. "You know, he really looked up to you," he said.

Don't, Roger wanted to say. The truth is I bullied him, the poor devil.

"By the way," Roger asked, "who are these letters going to?"

"The mayor and members of the library board. The press of course." George looked him in the eye. "And you."

"Get out of here," Roger growled. But he smiled as he closed his office door. If these Harvard kids had to be down here messing in his town's business, at least he could make some use of them.

August 1960

Betsy Nolan, elegant in her spectator pumps, edged along the broken pavement of Wilson Street, peering at the house numbers, some of which were missing, some covered with honeysuckle. Her green paisley dress fell in soft folds from a patent leather belt. The wide collar emphasized her long, white neck, not yet marred by the folds that would come soon enough.

She didn't know this street, didn't know this part of town. She stumbled on a fragment of sidewalk and quickly righted herself. Staring at peeling paint and unswept walkways, she thought, absent-mindedly, that this will be a mixed neighborhood before too long.

To her relief, the house she was looking for, 157 Wilson, struck a happy contrast to the general state of disintegration surrounding it. Fresh looking off-white stucco, maroon wooden shutters, recently painted. No cobwebs, grass in front, a doorbell that worked. A stout, buxom woman appeared at the door. Her stone-white hair was piled up on her large head in a loose knot and glasses hung from a chain around her neck.

"Well hello, Mrs. Nolan," she said pushing open the screen door. "What a surprise."

The woman looked familiar. Did she know her?

"I'm Thelma Foster," the woman said. "I taught Bryce chemistry."

"Of course. Miss Foster. I'm so sorry. I . . ."

"Thelma. And don't worry. I've been retired so long nobody recognizes me. Come in."

"What a lovely room," Betsy said.

The sun streamed through the stained glass oval above the door, bounced off a glass coffee table, made blue and red patterns of light on the white walls, and burnished the room in a warm honey gold.

"Thank you. Mama did it all those years ago, and I found no cause to change it after she died." She motioned to a silk Wedgewood chair. "What can I do for you, Mrs. Nolan?"

"I'm sorry to bother you, but I was told a George Bradstreet was staying here."

"Who told you that?"

"A friend." Roger had let it slip that he knew where George was living. But he was adamant that no one suspect he had actually met the boy.

Miss Foster studied her for a minute. "Was it Liz?" she finally asked.

Liz? Was she mixed up in this? "A friend said he was here," Betsy repeated. "Would it be possible for me to see him?"

The old teacher hesitated. "Could I ask what this is about?"

"He was Bryce's friend. I'd like to talk to him."

"I see. Wait here a minute."

When the old lady returned, she motioned for Betsy to follow her down a dimly lit hallway to a roomy closed-in back porch, paneled in cedar. George Bradstreet jumped up from a wrought-iron chair.

"Mrs. Nolan!"

"Don't look so scared," she laughed. "It's a friendly visit."

"If you don't need me . . ." Miss Foster said and disappeared.

The bright sunlight streamed in from the wall of French doors, open to afternoon breezes and the smell of newly cut grass. A round oak table dominated the room with captain chairs pushed under it. Papers were stacked all over the table. The wood floor of the original porch was painted white.

"How are you managing?" Betsy asked. This was the first time she had seen him since he'd turned up at her house.

George's words spilled out. "Fine, thank you. We're writing letters, using some ideas the Senator gave me. But I'm being really careful, I want you to know that, so I don't get the Senator in trouble."

"I know," she said, settling into one of the captain chairs, "but that's not why I'm here."

George sat back down, watching her under thick eyebrows.

"I want to know about Bryce."

"Sure."

"I know he was unhappy."

He frowned.

She leaned forward.

"The truth. Tell me the truth."

"The truth? Okay. Nobody's happy in college, especially freshman year, especially at Harvard."

"I don't mean everybody. I mean my son. What was it like for *him*?"

"He was smart, like everybody there, but he wasn't very interested in his studies. Is that what you mean?"

"Go on."

"Look, Mrs. Nolan, the world is changing. I mean the Brown decision changed everything. School is just irrelevant. I think that's how Bryce felt. I know I did. Still do." His voice was excited.

"And the meetings you told me about, did they make you feel relevant?"

"Yes ma'am. We wanted to make a difference."

"What about Bryce?"

"He felt the same."

"He wanted to make a difference?"

"Sure. The 'cause' gave us something to believe in."

She smiled faintly. "The manifesto?"

"He would have told you about it, but he didn't want to upset his dad."

Betsy thought for a moment, then blurted out, "Then, how come he was drinking?"

"Ma'am?"

"You knew him, George. Why was he drinking?"

"Everybody was drinking."

She looked away, her face drained of color. "Not everybody ran a car into a tree." Why had they ever agreed to let him take that car to college?

"It was an accident."

"He was drunk."

"He'd had a drink or two."

"I saw the police report," she said. "They tried to keep it from me, but I saw it." Her gray-blue eyes were fixed on him.

George looked away. "He didn't drink at our meetings," he said. "That was going to save him."

The words shocked her. "Save him?"

George stood up. Betsy watched him as he circled the room, clearly agitated. He's trying to find a way to say it without hurting me, she thought. He stopped at the bank of French doors and looked out.

"He loved you both," he said.

"But he felt he was letting us down."

"I didn't say that," George said.

"But it's true."

"He loved you. Look, the meetings made him happy. We were happy, all of us."

George was looking away from her, out into the bright sunlight.

"I loved him," he said. "Not like that sounds. He was my friend."

She walked over to him, took hold of his sharp shoulders and turned him toward her.

"Thank you," she said.

"By the way," George said as she turned to leave the room. "Was it Liz?"

"Was what Liz?"

He looked confused. "How'd you find me? Was it Jess?"

Liz again? And Jess? Florine's son? "What do you mean?"

"Look, Mrs. Nolan, forget I said anything."

She looked at him closely. "Is Jess involved in this?"

"I don't know."

"Of course you do."

"Look, don't say anything to the Senator. Please."

"I know that," Betsy said. "Take care of yourself, George."

As she turned to leave, George said, "Bryce thought you would agree with him." He swept his arm over the table, piled high with papers. "About all this. He said it many times. Said you couldn't do anything because of the Senator, but Bryce believed you'd understand."

"I haven't been very good at it so far," she said, her voice hoarse. Bryce, her own Bryce, had believed she'd understand. And she hadn't. Her head hurt from holding back tears.

As she picked her way over broken concrete on the way back home, she thought, that dull old chemistry teacher understood. Who would have guessed? And Jess. Florine's son. Florine must know. Working every day in the Senator's house. And Liz? What was *she* up to? It almost made her laugh.

Liz softly opened the door to her mother's room and tiptoed in. Taking a nap? No. Instead her mother was sitting in the rocking chair by the window, staring out. Good.

"Where've you been, honey?" Betsy asked without turning around.

"Seems like I haven't seen you for days."

Liz pulled up a footstool. "You know, Mama. Daddy got me that summer job at Johnsons, selling shoes."

"How's that coming along?"

"Lots of sweaty feet."

Betsy smiled. "Florine says you haven't been home for dinner."

She'd noticed? That was new. "I've been eating at that hamburger place with friends."

"What friends?"

What's she getting at? "You know, high school friends."

"I see."

"See what?"

"Well," Betsy paused. "I thought you might be involved in what they call the 'movement'."

Liz stiffened. "What are you talking about, Mama?"

Betsy looked at her daughter for the first time. "I paid George Bradstreet a visit last week," she said.

"You did what?" Was this possible?

"At Miss Foster's. She seemed to think *you* told me where he lived."

Liz didn't know what to say. She'd been so careful.

"You visited George? At Miss Foster's?"

"I wanted to know more . . . about Bryce," Betsy said. "I'm beginning to think I don't know much about either of my children."

Liz looked away from her mother, out the window. The grass stood stiff, yellow under the harsh August sun. The leaves on the maple hung dry, ready to drop with the first wind of fall.

Betsy hesitated for a minute as if she were trying to figure out what to say. "Are you working with George?"

Might as well get it over with. "Yes ma'am."

"Doing what?"

"Typing. Keeping records."

"Records?"

"They're going all over town with a petition to reopen the library."

"*You're* doing that?"

"Of course not," Liz said quickly. "Daddy would kill me. But they need a record of the petitions, how many people are signing, how many are refusing to sign, what neighborhoods they're in, that kind of thing." Liz sounded excited.

"Who's *they*?"

"For the lawsuit."

"Does your daddy know?"

"That I'm involved, I sure hope not."

Betsy paused. "How did you get started in this?"

Liz was relieved. Her mother didn't sound angry or accusing, just puzzled. Maybe even interested. But she couldn't get Florine in trouble.

"Somebody told me Miss Foster was helping open the library."

"Why didn't you tell me?"

She almost said, I didn't think you'd be interested, but stopped herself.

Betsy lightly touched her daughter's arm. "I wish you wouldn't keep all this a secret from me."

Liz looked at her mother for the first time and smiled. "I'm protecting you."

Betsy laughed. "From your father?"

Liz nodded.

October 1960

It was almost ten o'clock when Roger thought he heard a knock at the kitchen door. He peered out into the dark and saw somebody tall standing there.

"Mr. Nolan, I needs to talk to you." Florine looked directly at him, her eyes boring into his.

"Come in." What could she want?

When he had closed the door behind her, she said, "It's my boy."

Roger took a deep breath. Thank God. It wasn't Betsy. She'd seemed so much better recently, but she wasn't out of the woods.

"They got him in the jail."

"For what?" He remembered a small boy, shy, his thin brown arm hanging onto his mama. How old was he now?

"Some kids from the high school came by tonight. Said the police had Jess."

He must be a teenager by now. Getting into trouble already. "What'd he do?"

"They said he was disturbing the peace."

Roger sat down heavily on a kitchen stool. Why was she coming to him? She knew he couldn't get involved.

"Have you talked to him?"

"No sir. I went to the jail but they say he can't have no visitors."

"I'm sure they'll let you see him later."

Florine seemed to grow taller. She looked straight at him with wet eyes. "Mr. Nolan, I want you to get him out of there."

That's all he needed. He could see the headlines. Nolan backs protest movement. Gets agitator out of jail.

"You know I can't do that."

"They beating up boys in there," she said.

"That's just talk, Florine. The out of town press makes up that stuff to sell newspapers. Don't believe it."

"I seen the bruises myself. I seen the blood."

"When?"

"Last week. Not Jess. Other boys."

She was right, of course. He'd tried to talk to the Chief, told him it was hurting the town's reputation, which as a State Senator was his concern. But that good old boy just denied it. "Hell," he'd said, "we ain't laying a hand on 'em. We're only asking questions. Sons of bitches are lying."

"Look, Florine," he said. "I'd like to help, but my hands are tied." The easy cliché embarrassed him.

She turned away. "I know all bout that, sir." He leaned forward to hear her, her voice was so soft. "It was crazy to come here asking you. I could get myself fired. But he's my boy. He might be out there protesting, but he's not breaking the law. That's the God's truth, Mr. Nolan."

He sat there, gazing at her skinny back, silently cursing her for locking him into this strait-jacket. The newspapers were all over this goddamn business. If they found out Senator Nolan's maid was somehow part of it, he'd have to do something. Fire the maid for sure. And that's the last thing he wanted to do; he'd have hell to pay from Betsy and Liz. And if he pulled strings to get her boy out of jail and somebody found out, it would be even worse. He didn't want to think about that.

"I'm sorry, Florine," he said.

"You mighty smart, Mr. Nolan. That's why I come here."

He smiled. "Not that smart." But it got him to thinking about Police Chief Williams and how he'd pulled his butt out of the fire several years ago when the Chief got a little over zealous in his search and seizure practices. Roger had quietly, effectively put an end to an investigation and the Chief owed him one and knew it. But was this the time to play that card?

"Go on home, Florine. The jails are overflowing right now. They'll have to let your boy out in a day or two."

"But they'll charge him, and the judge will send him back."

They were both standing now, facing each other. "Look, Florine, there's a possibility he could get out without any charges against him. If that happens, we never had this conversation. Do you understand?"

"Yes sir. Thank you."

"I haven't done anything."

"Yes sir."

After she'd gone, Roger headed up to bed and found Betsy standing at the top of the stairs.

"What are you doing out here, sweetheart?"

"I heard you talking to somebody."

"It was Florine. She was just leaving. Go on back to bed."

"What's Florine doing here at this hour? It's about Jess, isn't it?"

"What do you know about Jess?"

"Nothing. I'm guessing."

Roger put his arm around Betsy's shoulders and started walking her back to her bedroom.

"He's in trouble, isn't he?" she said.

Roger stopped abruptly. Betsy turned to face him.

"I'm only guessing, but Jess is just the right age to be out there protesting. And the police are rounding up kids like him right and left and hauling them off to jail."

"That's what the papers say."

"Come on, Roger. You know it's true. And Florine is asking you to help Jess, isn't she?"

"How do you know . . ."

"I'm right, aren't I?"

She's so smart, he thought, she's always been smarter than anybody.
He nodded.

"You have to help her."

"I can't."

"Yes you can."

"Go to bed."

"Only if you'll promise to help her."

"Go to bed," he said again, and turned to leave. But she was smiling. She knows, he thought. She knows me better than anybody in the whole world.

The next evening when Florine opened her front door, she found Jess sprawled out on his mattress. Asleep.

"Thank you, sweet Jesus," she whispered and sat down on the floor next to him. Rocking back and forth, she ran her fingers lightly over his bare arms, over his scrawny neck, through his tightly curled hair, feeling for cuts, looking for bruises.

Then he was throwing his arms around her, this large almost man who was her boy. Squeezing her so tight she had to pull herself away to catch her breath.

"I was so scared. Mama, I was so scared." Over and over.

Finally, "How'd you get out?"

"I was in this cell with a bunch of other guys and this cop opened the door and yelled out, 'Which one of you assholes is Jess?' Scared me to death cause they been calling boys out and beating on 'em. Somebody pointed at me. So I stood up. 'Come on,' the cop said. Next thing I knew, I was out the jailhouse door and heading home."

"Nobody told you why they were letting you go?"

"No ma'am."

"They say anything about charges?"

"No'm. Said I was free."

They struggled to their feet, still tangled up together.

"You hungry?"

"What do you think?"

They sat together at the metal-topped table, eating warmed over spoonbread, drinking milk.

"You gotta stop," Florine finally said.

"Stop what?"

"Don't play dumb with me. Next time you be staying in that jail."

"You talked to him, didn't you, Mama?"

"Who?"

"You know who."

"No."

"You not going to get fired, are you?"

She smiled. "Not if you keep clear of those protests."

"I mean to," he said. But she knew how young he was, how innocent, even now, and she could only pray he'd listen to her this time.

The following evening after work, when Roger opened the front door, he found Florine inside waiting for him.

"My boy's home," she said.

"Well, that's good news."

"Thank you."

"What for?"

"I just wanted to say it."

"Well, thank *you* for all the help you give this family," he said.

"You're welcome," she said.

February 1961

Betsy stood perfectly still, staring at a stack of letters on the table. Her hair was almost entirely gray now, and there were lines on her broad forehead and along the sides of her eyes. Since her first visit to Thelma Foster's house, she had come several times with Liz. She told herself she was keeping an eye on her daughter, making sure she was safe, but in fact Betsy was becoming more immersed in George's work, editing letters, tallying petitions, making suggestions for his meetings in the black churches. George was now working for the NAACP all over Virginia. But his focus for the moment was on the Spotswood library.

Thelma Foster reached over with spindly fingers and picked up a letter and handed it to Betsy.

Betsy ran her eyes over the letter.

"Do you think this will do it?" the teacher asked, watching Betsy with hooded green eyes.

"You got a better idea?" George asked her.

"No."

"Look," he said. "None of those Neanderthals actually wants to live in a city without a public library. It's embarrassing. That's why we're pushing the risk-of-losing-business angle. It's the argument Mr. Nolan's using with the mayor to get a settlement."

"Preaching won't do it," the old lady said.

"We're not preaching. We're pointing out the facts."

"And the facts are?"

"No commercial enterprise will look at a town without a library."

Betsy was still staring at the letter. "The facts," she suddenly said. "Here's one. It's not about the books."

"Huh?"

"No one actually minds them reading books. At least that's what the mayor says."

"Just not in our library," Miss Foster said.

Betsy turned to face the window. Outside dark limbs of a maple were silhouetted against the gray sky.

"What they don't want is the mixing," she murmured. "That's the important fact. We keep forgetting it."

They both stared at her.

"It's chairs," she said.

They waited, puzzled.

"If you can't sit down in the library . . . ."

George finished her sentence. "You can't stick around to mix." He started laughing, a high whinny of a laugh. Betsy realized she'd never heard him laugh before.

"Brilliant," he said. "You get your books and you go home."

Betsy smiled. "It's just an idea."

June 1961

Roger waved the newspaper in the air.

Betsy sat on the rose velvet sofa, watching him, her shoulders, as always, straight. Her slender, veined hands rested in her lap.

He pointed to the headline, *Library Opens With No Chairs, No Fanfare* and began to read aloud.

The Library in the Memorial Mansion opened its doors today for the first time since April 1960, when Mayor John Watson was forced to close it to prevent racial conflict. The reopening of the library resulted from the settlement of a lawsuit brought against the city by the NAACP. According to the terms of the settlement, all chairs have been removed from the library premises.

The library opened quietly without disturbance. Contacted in his office, Senator Roger Nolan stated, "I am pleased we have resolved this unfortunate lawsuit in a peaceful manner. My family and I intend to patronize the library on a regular basis."

"Chairs," Roger said, "Just brilliant. Wish I'd thought of it."

September 1961

Roger knocked softly on his wife's bedroom door.

"Can I talk to you?"

She opened the door wide and smiled. "Come in."

"The governor just called."

Betsy's smile vanished. She nodded in the direction of the green damask daybed and eased herself into the rocker.

"He wants me to run in the '62 election."

"For?"

"The Senate."

"You're in the Senate."

"The U.S. Senate."

Her smile was back. "Congratulations. I can see the library settlement paid off."

But Roger wasn't smiling. He was watching her carefully. "You know why I'm here."

"Yes." Of course. The inevitable. And she dreaded it with her whole being.

"The Senate is big, you know that. I have to be seen and heard. Every day. For the next year. And if my wife doesn't show up now and then, people will ask questions."

"What exactly do you want?"

"I need you next to me when I make speeches. Not every time, of course. And I need you at fundraisers."

"Is the governor writing the speeches?"

"Of course not."

"You know what I mean."

"You mean, do I have to support the governor's stand on school segregation?" he asked.

She nodded.

"Jesus, Betsy. Be realistic."

"I am realistic. I'd like to help you. But I can't. And you know it."

Roger stood up, reached for her hand and pulled her to her feet. They stood facing each other, not touching.

"It means I can't run."

"I don't think so."

"They'll say we're estranged. Or that you're depressed or worse."

"I'm not depressed. I *was* worse. But not now."

"Then why can't you do this for me?"

"It would destroy me."

He paused a minute. Then, "You're too strong for that. But if you don't, it might destroy me."

"No it won't. You're too clever. You'll figure out some story. I'm no longer hibernating; I'm back in the world. I'm working on Bryce's Scholarship Fund. Use that. Use my grief; that's always available." She gave a small laugh.

"You'll at least come to fundraisers?"

"Only if they're local and only if they don't involve segregation politics."

He laughed. "I'll see if I can organize one." He took her hands and pulled her to him. She felt his chest, hard after all these years, his stomach, flat. He'd been exercising. How nice it would be to stay there, breathe in the mix of fresh laundry and aftershave.

"You know," he murmured in her ear, "that I agree with you."

She pushed him away. "When you say things like that I get crazy. I know you used to agree. That's why I can't watch you make those awful speeches about 'mixing the races'."

"You know I have to support the Governor's position to get elected in this state."

"Yes, and I know you can't resist running for office. I just don't have to be a part of it."

"But you are."

"Not anymore. Every time you make one of those feel-good southern speeches, all I can think about is Bryce."

"Don't!" Roger moaned.

"We need to talk about it and we never do. You know, as well as I, that he was fighting against your governor . . . ."

"Stop, goddammit. You're using him against me."

"I hate what you stand for."

Roger glared at her, his eyes dark, fierce. "What do you mean by that?" he hissed. "You know what I stand for, what you and I have always stood for."

"And what's that?" she asked.

"A world that's fair and equal for everyone."

"You should hear yourself, Roger." Her voice was soft, tired. "That's just cant. You know you haven't believed that for a long time."

"I still do believe it," he said. "But I can't do anything about it if I'm not elected. We're stuck with a losing cause here in the South, but somebody smart's going to find a way out. And that's what I'm good at."

"I wish I could believe you."

"You don't have to believe me, just don't hate me."

She looked into his eyes. "I don't hate you."

He put his arms around her slender shoulders and pressed her against him. "I used to be good at loving," he said. "I was good at loving you."

"I know," she said, pulling away.

"I still do."

She looked up at him, her college sweetheart, handsome still, earnest, his dark eyes begging her. She knew every contour of his back, could feel, this minute, the strength of his arms, knew he loved her.

"But love doesn't save us anymore," she said, "it died with . . . . "

"Don't," he cried.

"Running for Congress saves you. The Scholarship Fund saves me. I think, all things considered, we're lucky."

"So do we have a deal?"

"I'm here, I'm your wife, through the election. But be careful not to let the press near me."

"What do you mean, through the election?" His voice was sharp.

"We'll see."

"No. It's not worth it." He pulled her close, held her hard against him. "Nothing's worth losing you. I'll tell the Governor, no. That's final." When she didn't respond, he kissed her forehead, then turned and left the room.

But she knew it wasn't final. He would run. He couldn't help himself. After that? Who knew? Right now it didn't matter.

She felt alive. That's what mattered.

October 1962

Liz stood at the back of the crowd, peering around the heads in front of her, straining to see the speaker.

"Let me tell you, I am *proud* to be a Virginian. Just like every one of *you*. Proud of this state. *Our* state. And you know? We have the right to be proud. George Washington was a Virginian; Thomas Jefferson was a Virginian; James Madison was a Virginian. Virginians fought the American Revolution for our right to independence. And today we're still fighting for our independence."

The crowd cheered.

Liz tried to tell herself it wasn't him.

She'd come up to Farmville, Virginia, this October morning, with a busload of students from Duke. She'd been riding the Freedom Bus every weekend since she'd joined the Students for Racial Equality, visiting towns all over North Carolina and southern Virginia, picketing segregated movie houses and restaurants and swimming pools, carrying signs. It felt scary and she was always worried she'd run into somebody from home, although how could she? At the same time, it felt right to be on those picket lines. Bryce would have been there. She imagined him, her big brother, walking just ahead of her, a bag full of petitions slung over his shoulder. Like when he was a paperboy.

They'd wanted her to go with them to Spotswood. That town's as redneck as they come, they'd said. Schools still lily white. And you know it inside out. But, brave as she felt on all those picket lines, she wasn't ready to face her hometown. Even more, she didn't want to make trouble for her daddy.

Farmville wasn't home. The students planned to picket the all-white private high school the county had been supporting since 1959 when it had closed the public schools to avoid desegregation.

As they drove into town, they saw a large crowd gathered in front of what looked like a courthouse. Everybody was white and there was a lot of yelling.

"Okay," Dickie Sutherlin, the group leader, shouted. "Let's check it out."

Liz waded into the crowd behind Dickie, edging herself past the swollen bellies of middle-age men in plaid flannel shirts open at the collar. The men were clapping and hollering.

The amplified voice broke through the din. "Our state has the right under the United States Constitution to make its own decisions about public education. You in this town, in this great Prince Edward County, are fighting for that Constitutional right."

It *was* him. No mistaking. Liz turned and started inching her way back through the crowd.

But Dickie was raising his fist in the air and yelling, "Integrate!" in a shrill voice that cut through all the cheering, and the other students started yelling with him. Liz felt a hand on her shoulder jerking her so hard she fell back into a mass of arms and legs. She was breathing hard, trying not to cry, when the area around her suddenly cleared and a policeman, his round face dirty with sweat, yanked her wrists in front of her with one large fleshy hand and pulled her to her feet. He held a billy club in his other hand. "Let me go!" she screamed as she twisted back and forth, but he just glowered at her.

But then he suddenly twisted his head in the direction of the speaker's stand. She followed his gaze. Her father had stopped speaking and was walking down the stairs, wading into the crowd toward the policemen, who stood frozen, watching.

Liz started to call to him, to acknowledge him, to let him rescue her. To cry out the word, Daddy. But there were her friends, their wrists in handcuffs, watching her with puzzled frowns, waiting to see what she would do.

Liz looked straight at her father and began to sing in a low voice. "We shall overcome. We shall overcome." Then her friends joined in, louder and louder. "We shall overcome some day ay ay ay."

134 / Nancy Bourne

"Let 'em go," her father said to the policeman who was holding her wrists. "They're just kids. I don't want trouble from some college."

The tension broke. The fat cop let go of Liz. Her fellow students rubbed their wrists as the handcuffs came off. Roger Nolan squared his shoulders, marched back to the speaker's stand, and picked up the microphone.

"We're supposed to be at that private school," Liz said. "Let's get out of here." And to her relief they followed her.

What in the hell was Liz doing here? It wasn't easy to make these damn speeches, encouraging these rednecks to defy the Supreme Court and keep their schools closed. He hated it. Hated every minute of it. Surely she knew that. Knew he had no choice. If he wanted to be elected, these speeches were mandatory. And he wanted to be a United States Senator. That was real power. But she was too naïve, this daughter of his, too full of misplaced idealism. She couldn't, or wouldn't, see that once he was a Senator, he could work behind the scenes, work with Virginia, get all the goddamn schools back open. Like he did with the library.

He'd been warming up his audience, watching the faces smile, watching the eyes follow him, watching the heads nodding at him. Then out of the corner of his eye, he'd seen some movement in the crowd, heard someone yelling. A disturbance. Police. It broke the rhythm of his speech. Made him stop, assess the damage. It was okay. He'd been here before; he knew the drill. Give 'em a gracious smile. A calm voice. Nod at the policemen to step aside.

Then, "Come on up to the platform, young man. Let me finish my speech and then you can give yours."

It had always worked before. Rabble rousers liked the comfortable anonymity of a crowd. They backed away from standing up front.

And then he'd seen her. Some cop pulling at her. No time to think. He'd had to rescue her.

But she'd rescued *him*. She'd looked right at him and started in on that singing. If she had called out to him, called his name, or let the police drag her off, he would have been lost. It would have been on the front page of every morning newspaper: *Nolan Sides with Protesters against Farmville Police. Protects His Integrationist Daughter.* His campaign would have been over. But she'd started singing, and in that split second he knew she didn't *want* to be rescued. She wanted to make a statement, poor misguided creature.

So he'd called off the stupid cops, then turned back to the podium and picked up his microphone.

"Looks like we have some folks who don't agree with us," he said with a smile. "Well, they have a right to their point of view. And we have a right to ours."

The crowd cheered. They were with him.

"They don't have a right to disturb the peace, though."

More cheers.

That did the trick. Liz and her crowd turned tail. Disappeared. Thank God.

He'd have time afterwards to square it with the police, who'd have questions. The Governor would take care of the press.

Meanwhile, Liz. What in God's name was she doing, running around the country with a bunch of trouble makers? He'd make sure it didn't happen again.

SENATOR RUNNING FOR OFFICE DENIES SON'S ACTIVISM

State Senator Roger Nolan put to rest on Thursday rumors that his son Bryce had been involved in the integrationist movement before his tragic death in 1957. A reporter for the Washington Post raised the question during a speech Mr. Nolan was giving in Alexandria, Virginia, as part of his campaign for the U. S. Senate.

"Wasn't your son a member of the "Integrate the Schools" movement while he was at Harvard?" the reporter asked.

"My family is off limits," Mr. Nolan politely replied.

"Not if your family opposes your views on integration," the reporter persisted.

"My son Bryce died three years ago in a tragic automobile accident," the Senator said, "and I refuse to answer any questions about him or any of my family."

"Senator Nolan, I have right here a document signed by a Bryce Nolan of Harvard University stating his opposition to segregated schools."

"I don't know what you have, and I don't care," the Senator replied, his voice rising in anger. "My son Bryce signed no such document. He was just eighteen years old when he was killed. A young boy, immature. He didn't know his own mind. He was behind in school and too busy catching up to be involved in politics."

The reporter, however, would not be silenced. "So you deny your son's involvement in the integrationist movement?"

"Yes I do," the Senator stated.

The day before in Farmville, Virginia, out-of-state student agitators raised their fists and booed Senator Nolan, in an attempt to disrupt a campaign speech. As the local police closed in to disperse the students, the Senator waded bravely into the crowd and calmed the students, who departed peacefully.

After the disruption, Mr. Nolan returned to the podium to give a rousing speech in support of Massive Resistance.

"You seen the paper?" Jess handed Florine the morning edition of the Spottsville Dispatch.

"I seen it."

"I told you."

"Told me what?"

"He's a racist."

Florine sat down heavily on the wooden bench, the newspaper in her lap.

"He's lost," she said. "He's got some good inside him. I got evidence for that. But he's lost."

ACKNOWLEDGMENTS

First of all, I am grateful to the literary journals which published the following stories included in this collection: "Going Under" in *The Carolina Quarterly*, "The Columbia" in *The South Carolina Review*, "Massive Resistance," in *The Long Story*, "Dirty Dora" in *Thin Air Magazine*, "Memorial Mansion" in *Persimmon Tree*, "Sterling Silver" in *Midway Journal*, "Drawing Lily" and "We Gather Together" in *Forge Journal*, "Faster Than A Roller Coaster" in *Poydras Review*.

Next I want to thank all of my writer friends who have read and critiqued the stories and made them better. First and foremost is Daniel Coshnear, author and teacher, who read and critiqued the collection, helped me shape the stories into a book and encouraged me at every step. And I am so grateful to the following writing group members and cherished friends: JoAnne Rosen, Linda Saldana, Wray Cotterill, Richard Gustafson, Karen Pierce Gonzalez, Marko Fong, Eve Goldberg, Amanda Yskamp, Sarah Amador, Marie Narlock, JoAnne Tillermans, Dom Lim, Esther Gulli, Barbara Jordan, Steven Wightman, and Richard Kleiner.

Thank you to Laurie Ann Doyle, for helping me get started on this project and encouraging me to follow through. A very special thank you to Tom Parker, my first real writing teacher, who taught me how to shape a short story and how to listen to criticism.

I am particularly grateful to Kimberly Verhines, my editor at Stephen F. Austin State University Press, who picked my collection from the multitude of submissions, encouraged me at every stage, and made my dream of publishing a book a reality.

Finally, I thank my son Michael Bourne, whose book *Blithedale Canyon* is scheduled for publication in 2022, for discovering my secret life of story writing and encouraging it in every way. I thank my children Randy Bourne and Molly Bourne for being the wonderful, supportive people they are. And for husband, Henry, who has encouraged my writing and me through all the years. Words don't begin to express my deepest gratitude.

9 781622 884087